Time Jumpers

Book Three

the
FUTURE
is
unknown

James Valentine

Aladdin Paperbacks
New York London Toronto Sydney

FOR ROY

ALADDIN PAPERBACKS
An imprint of Simon & Schuster Children's Publishing Division
1230 Avenue of the Americas, New York, NY 10020
Copyright © 2004 by James Valentine
Originally published in Australia as *JumpMan Rule #3: See Rule One!!!* in 2004 by
Random House Australia Pty Ltd
Published by arrangement with Random House Australia Pty Ltd
All rights reserved, including the right of reproduction in whole
or in part in any form.
ALADDIN PAPERBACKS and related logo are registered trademarks of
Simon & Schuster, Inc.
Designed by Mike Rosamilia
The text of this book was set in Aldine 401BT.
Manufactured in the United States of America
First Aladdin Paperbacks edition August 2007
2 4 6 8 10 9 7 5 3 1
Library of Congress Cataloging-in-Publication Data
Valentine, James.
[Jumpman, rule #3 see rule one!!!]
The future is unknown / James Valentine.—1st U.S. ed.
p. cm.—(Timejumpers ; bk. 3)
Summary: With Quincy Carter One on the loose somewhere in time, TimeJumping
supposedly not safe anymore, and history starting to Unhappen, Jules and Gen
are once again called upon to help correct the past.
ISBN-13: 978-0-689-87354-6
ISBN-10: 0-689-87354-9
[1. Time travel—Fiction. 2. Science fiction.] I. Title.
PZ7.V252Jw 2007
[Fic]—dc22
2006038337

chapter one
FREE TIME

"Hey, that's so free you came!" yelled Max, punching Jules hard on the arm and swinging into the seat beside him.

"Sure," replied Jules, trying to look like the punch on the arm hadn't hurt.

"It's gonna be really free," continued Max. "We get to Blast, and then I'll show you how to slide a throbbing beast of a machine through a hairpin, up a mountain zigzag—"

And Max vroomed in his seat, changing imaginary gears as though he were not in a bus chugging slowly through traffic but hurtling in a Subaru WRX all-wheel drive along forest roads toward another victory in the World Rally Championship.

1

Not that Max had ever driven a Subaru WRX, although he had sat in one once in a showroom for a dare, before the salesguy chased them out. But he did have Xbox, did have World Rally Championship software, and was a regular at Blast—the game parlor in the city, with the big screens and the linked machines, that Max and his friends went to most weekends.

Jules looked out the window. He'd never been to Blast, and he wasn't quite sure why he was going now. He was restless. He couldn't settle into anything at the moment. He was nervy and felt strange all the time. He was tired. He was getting headaches. He was on edge. He needed a change. He needed to do something different and shake things up.

"Hey, I wonder if I've still got fourth fastest on WRC," said Max, not really wondering about it at all, just saying it to let Jules know that he did have fourth fastest on WRC.

Jules stopped looking out the window and turned to Max.

"What's with 'free'?" he asked. "You keep saying stuff is 'free.' 'Hey, that's free.' Where did 'free' come from?"

"Exactly!" said Max, grabbing Jules's arm. "Where do all the cool words come from? Where did 'cool' come from? Who started saying 'awesome'? Who decided that 'gay' meant, like, not gay but, you know, kind of gay?"

"What do you mean, 'who'? There's no 'who.' Someone doesn't decide this stuff, it just happens."

Max shook his head. "I don't think so. It's like who starts a Mexican wave, you know? Someone does. Well, this is the same, I reckon. Someone starts saying this stuff, and then some other kid, and then their friends say it, and then it's everywhere."

"So you're just gonna use this all the time, and then what? Stand up and claim to be the first?" asked Jules.

Max shrugged. "I don't know. See what happens. I got others," he offered.

"Really? Not just 'free'?"

Max shook his head. "Try this. You ready?"

"Yeah, I'm ready."

Max turned to Jules, looked at him intently, and said, "Marvelous."

"Marvelous?"

Max nodded.

"Yeah, see, it's like 'excellent.' Kind of old fashioned, but then if we start using it, it'll sound really cool. Uh, free."

"Marvelous," said Jules. "I don't know, just sounds like my aunty."

"Yeah, maybe. Okay, try this one." Max licked his lips

and cleared his throat and then pronounced, "Spiff."

"Spiff? What's that mean? Is it good or bad?"

"Not sure yet," replied Max. "Could be either. What do you think?"

"I think it sounds like something you wipe off. Where are you getting all this stuff from?" Jules was amazed at Max. His talk was usually just dirty. He had a mountain of obscene misinformation from his older brothers, and that formed the basis of his usual conversation. Here he was inventing new words. It wasn't like him at all.

Max shrugged. "I dunno. Someone has to do it. Why not us?"

The bus was coming into the city, and as it maneuverd through the traffic, Jules breathed in deeply and sat up a little straighter. This wasn't so bad. He and Max were doing a fair impression of a couple of kids who might be friends. He could spend the afternoon at Blast racing cars, blowing away terrorists and aliens by the millions, it'd be good.

And maybe, for a moment, he could stop thinking about Theo. About TimeJumping. Maybe for an afternoon he could pretend that Theo wasn't about to Jump in and whip him and Gen away to someplace where they might be killed. Instead he could play some machines where being killed was part of the game, and then the game was over.

Their stop was next. Time to get over Theo. Time to move on from TimeJumping. Theo was three thousand years away. The nearest JumpMan was three thousand years away. It wasn't going to happen again, and it was time to get back into now. The here and now. The now that is here and the here that is now. And it was time to stop thinking like that as well.

Oh, I don't know. I like it when you think like that, said Jules's brain.

It's not me that thinks like that. It's you.

I am you. You keep pretending like I'm someone else. I'm not.

You're not me. I'm me. And I'm someone who doesn't talk to his brain.

You do.

Don't. Watch me.

Do.

Jules didn't reply. He'd been talking to his brain for years now, and he had to admit that his brain was often quite helpful, but he just felt as though he was too old to still be doing it. It was like keeping your teddy bear.

The bus stopped and they jumped off. Max yelled at him. "Come on! Let's go. It'll be grinding."

"Yeah, free," Jules yelled back, and punched Max on

the arm. They ran up the street toward Blast, bashing into pedestrians and then barging on, oblivious to their angry looks.

Blast was easy to find. You heard it before you saw it. Max whooped as they ran inside, and leapt straight onto World Rally Championship.

"Perfect timing! Hey, I'm still number four! THE DETONATOR. That's me! It looks really free. What do you want to drive?"

Jules wished he was a better game player, but what the hell, it was time to learn. When his mom and dad had been together, they'd thought he was too young to have an Xbox, or even a Game Boy. When they split and he went with his mom, Angela, to live up north, she'd had no money and thought he should be learning to dance or play the flute.

For his birthday she'd given him a yoga mat. "This generation needs to find its serenity, not sit in front of yet another screen and model yet more violent behavior," she'd said as she climbed with him to the top of the local mountain so that they could watch the dawn together on the morning of his birthday. She'd made him meditate before she'd given him the purple mat, tied up with hemp rope. Then she'd sung him a song she'd written about him. He'd rather have had the Box.

When he'd come back to live with his dad, Jules had hinted a bit and then asked, and Tony had said sure, maybe they could get one and play together, but somehow he hadn't quite got around to it yet.

"Frankly," said his dad, who'd also been pretty strange since the last TimeJumping episode, "you know I'm proud of you whatever you do. But boys need to expend energy. You were good at karate. Why not get back into that instead of spending yet more time looking at a little screen?"

Jules couldn't quite see how learning to kick someone in the head was better than kicking them on the screen with a joystick, but as yet no amount of discussion had produced a machine in his living room.

That was part of the reason he loved TimeJumping. He could do it. He was good at it. He just wished the guys could see him do it, and he wished it would help him now as he crashed his Peugeot yet again, then watched Max's Subaru WRX sprint off ahead.

"Free! Heading for PB. Woohoo!" yelled Max. "Watch and learn, my friend, watch and learn!"

Max had become very painful in here. Jules swung his steering wheel and tried to get back on the road. His wheels spun, he headed off, he was airborne, and he smashed into a tree.

"GAME OVER GAME OVER GAME OVER GAME OVER GAME OVER."

Once would have been enough.

Max continued alone, sprinting up through the forest, spraying dirt into the trees.

Jules got up and wandered around. There were three or four other kids that he knew, and he nodded at them, but their attention was fixed on the screens in front of them. *Fair enough,* thought Jules. No one comes to Blast for conversation.

Blast was three floors of ear-jarring action. There were machines everywhere. Kids were dancing in front of them, playing drums on them, mixing up dance tracks on them. They were racing every vehicle ever made: rally cars, Formula One, V-8s, rocket bikes, trucks, and speedboats. They were in forests in Finland, at Monte Carlo and Daytona, on drag strips, and zipping by tropical islands and coral reefs.

If you didn't want to race something, perhaps you'd like to kill something. Kids were blasting alien ships out of the heavens by the millions. They were taking on thousands of troops or defending themselves against brutish assailants using knives, samurai swords, whizzing bits of metal, and martial arts moves not possible in real life. If that failed, they were mowing them down with

Magnums and Glocks, bazookas and machine guns, stun bombs and grenades, rocket launchers and guided missiles. They had pulse guns, ray guns, and lasers, but still the enemy kept on coming, leaping out from behind buildings, dropping from impossible heights, marching on inexorably, stony faced and lethal.

Once you tired of killing and maiming, there were plenty of more relaxing options. You could shoot some hoops with Michael Jordan, return some serves from Lleyton Hewitt, head for a goal with David Beckham, or play eighteen holes with Tiger Woods. The world was available if the computer had enough memory to handle the graphics, the sound effects, and the seemingly infinite levels of the game.

For two dollars you could conquer the universe or dance with Britney Spears. Maybe you would, like Max, reach the ultimate goal of digitally inscribing yourself on the machine—your initials, your nickname in this world clearly outlined in bold letters alongside your prodigious score for others to marvel at and attempt to beat.

Two dollars could buy you an hour if you knew what you were doing. But if you were like Jules, two dollars bought you about a minute-and-a-half's worth of fun before you were thrown out, looking like a total loser.

So Jules did the same as the other kids who couldn't

play. He started watching the experts. Hoping that by watching he'd pick up what to do. While watching, it was important that he adopt the right stance. He tried to suggest by the look on his face, the angle of his head, and the slant of his body that he was actually a champion at whatever he was observing; he could play anytime he wanted to, but right now he was just interested in the tactics employed by these lesser operators whom he could beat anytime he chose.

He just felt in the way.

Jules went up and down the three floors for a while. It wasn't really a place for spectators.

He went back to where Max had been tearing up half of Scandinavia in his WRX. Max had gone.

That's funny, thought Jules. *I haven't seen him on anything else. Must have missed him.*

Jules went and sat down at a white plastic table that was pretending it was a café, and spent some of his money on a can of Coke and some limp-looking french fries that were struggling to stay upright in their jaunty cardboard box.

A bored attendant wearing earplugs heated up the food and gave him his change.

Jules bit into a french fry that was soggy and warm at one end and kind of raw at the other, and started regretting the entire afternoon. Max wasn't really his friend. He just liked having Jules around because Jules was now strangely cool. And now Max had gone off somewhere else.

Jules decided to go home. He'd half-risen from his seat when Max slipped out of a dark corner, fell against a wall, and slid slowly to the ground.

Jules leapt up and raced over to him.

Max was pale and clammy. He was shivering, and his eyes were wide open, staring at something in the middle distance. He had flecks of spit around his mouth, and he was shaking, almost convulsing. He sat up, looked at Jules, said, "I'm all right," and then threw up on the floor.

"Max!" yelled Jules. "Are you sick? What's wrong?"

Max straightened up, and the earplugged attendant came over and started yelling at them. "Get out! Now! You two! You drunk! Don't come back!"

"No!" protested Jules. "We're not drunk. He's sick. We need some help."

The attendant wasn't listening, he was pushing them outside.

Jules looked around for someone to assist them, but everyone kept blazing away and paid no attention to two kids getting thrown out.

Max slumped at the knees and fell against Jules.

Jules grabbed him before he collapsed completely, and then staggered outside with him.

Out on the street Max was still shaky on his feet. Jules was having trouble holding him up. The two of them staggered about, knocking into people, all of whom scowled and yelled at them to get out of the way.

Jules looked for a friendly face, but no luck. On a Saturday afternoon this part of town was full of kids with nothing to do, and adults who had to pass through this area did so with their heads down, ignoring everything. These kids could be on drugs, or want to mug them. Best to ignore them and get out of there. No one wanted to help.

Jules got Max into a doorway, and they both slumped down on the step.

Max closed his eyes and leaned his head back on the door.

"Woooow," he said quietly. "Wooooowwooooooo."

"Max! What happened to you?" asked Jules, still looking up and down the street in the hope that someone might come to their aid.

"Wooow. That was wild."

Jules looked closely at Max. He'd opened his eyes, but then he shut them again and moaned a bit more. He was kind of panting, but a little more color was returning to his face. He was twisting around on the step as though he couldn't really get comfortable.

"Oh, wooow. That was amazing," he said.

"What? What was amazing?"

Max slumped back again, opened his eyes, and looked at Jules.

"I've just been in a battle. I think I cut some guy's head off."

Jules stared at Max. What on Earth was he talking about?

"I was on a horse," Max continued. "I was in a long line of horses. It was cold, like it was just after dawn or something."

Jules was really starting to worry. This was serious. Max was delusional.

"We were on one side of a big open field. And across the field was another line of horses and all these guys with swords and shields. I was looking out through a little slit in my helmet, and I was wearing kind of like a metal shirt or something."

This was so bad. Max was raving.

"And then I heard a horn sound, and my horse took off. All the other horses did too, and we were charging across the field, and all the other guys on the other side of the field were charging toward us. I thought, *Oh, man, I better get my sword out.* And then I thought, *What the hell am I doing with a sword?* But there it was in my hand and I was swinging it up, and then there was a guy in front of me on his horse, and I swung my sword, and it was like hitting a golf ball or something. His head just flew off and there was a neck riding a horse, blood spurting out . . ."

Max got to about there and turned pale green. He looked like he was about to be sick again but stopped himself just in time.

"Max," said Jules. "Max, look at me. We've been at Blast. Is this some new machine you're talking about?"

"Yeah," said Max. "But it's not like any of the others. This is real. It wasn't a screen. I was, like, there! I could feel the horse. I could hear everything. I heard the guy scream. I could feel my sword cut into the skin and then it, like, really jarred. I must have hit his bones or something."

Max threw up this time.

A businessman dodged the spray and yelled at them. "Come on, boys! Just go home, will ya?"

Jules apologized and then turned his attention back to Max. "Max. Max, you okay?"

Max smiled weakly. "Not really. Can we just sit here for a while?"

"Sure. Take your time."

"Time. Yeah, that was it."

"That was what?" asked Jules.

"The game. It came up on a screen."

"Oh, so there was a screen?"

"Well, not really. It was kind of in your head. You put these things on and then you were just there."

"Just where?"

Max sat up a little and grabbed Jules by the arm.

"I was there, Jules. I was in the battle. You got to try it. It's unreal. It's better than anything else in there."

Max was getting a little excited. Jules didn't want him to be sick again, so he tried to calm him down.

"Okay, Max, okay. I'll try it. What's it called?"

"Something like TimeJumper, or TimeJump, or something like that."

Jules felt as though he'd been slapped across the face. A cold shock grabbed his stomach.

"TimeJump?" He held Max's gaze. "Did you say 'TimeJump'?"

"Yeah. I only saw it for a moment and then I was sitting on my horse in my chain mail—that's it. It was a chain mail shirt. I had a big sword—Adrick! My name was Adrick and I was riding for the king—"

"Yeah right, Max, just take it easy." Max was starting

15

to rise up from the step, and once again the busy crowd streaming by was starting to notice them and look at them like they were mad hoons.

He said 'TimeJump,' said Jules's brain.

I know. I heard him. Didn't I say I wasn't talking to you?

Well, how could he say 'TimeJump'? How does he know about it?

He doesn't.

He said it. He must.

It's just a game.

Doesn't sound like a game. Sounds like he TimeJumped.

Shut up. Go away.

I can help you.

But Jules didn't reply, and his brain slunk off to try to deal in its own way with this sudden news that TimeJumping was now a new game at Blast, next to Marine Commando and Crash Derby.

"Max. Can you walk again?" asked Jules.

"I think so," said Max.

He rose a little unsteadily but then took a few steps and he was fine. He took some deep breaths, shook his head, and then grinned a little at Jules.

"Let's go find the guy. You gotta try it."

Jules grabbed Max by the arm. "Guy? What guy?"

"I don't know. Some guy."

Jules stopped outside Blast. "What are you talking about, Max. What happened? What guy?"

"I was playing BlackHawk Patrol. I was on level thirteen—you know, where you have to fly down, like, a Chicago street, and there's the terrorists blasting at you—"

"Yeah, Max, not the game, the guy!" prompted Jules.

"That's what I'm telling you! The guy came and watched me. Put me off a bit. I reckon I could have taken out the sixteen fighter jets that came straight at me if he hadn't—"

"Max!"

"Oh yeah. So anyway, I finish. And he says, hi, did I want to try a brand-new game. He was the sales rep or something, and he was giving kids a free try. So we, like, go all the way upstairs and through this door and into this room. It felt odd, that room. Like you were there and not there at the same time. Anyway, I sit down, he kind of hooks me up, and that was it."

"What happened when you finished?"

"I don't know."

"You don't know?"

"I don't know! I was in the battle, and then I was with you. I didn't see him again."

Jules and Max went back into Blast, dodging around

the attendant who'd thrown them out earlier. They went up to the top floor.

There was no door.

"Can you see the guy?"

Max shook his head.

They headed back downstairs, and Jules felt a hand clamp down on his shoulder.

"I told you. You don't come in here! I don't want you in here. Get out!"

The attendant threw them out again.

They stumbled up the street and into a McDonald's. They sat down, and that was when Jules noticed the rusty red blotches on Max's hands.

"Max, what's that on your hands?"

Max frowned and looked at the red patches. Then he sniffed them. Then he got up and ran to the toilet.

It was a tough trip home. After Max had sniffed the blood on his hands, he'd gone into a kind of shock. Jules had followed him into the toilet, and Max had thrown up again and then spent ages trying to clean the spots off his hands.

They'd just missed their bus and then had to wait nearly an hour for another one.

Plenty of time to think.

Max had Jumped. No question. No one reacted like

that to a machine, to a computer game. Max had done something real. That was blood on his hands. And Max kept remembering more and more details of the battle he'd experienced. The smell of the horses, things he'd heard yelled out across the field, challenges and orders and prayers.

"So long as the Lord Our God is in heaven, we shall prevail!" he yelled in the street while they lined up for the bus. People moved away from them. He also started to remember who he'd been. He was Adrick, Son of Aymon. He was a peasant farmer, and one day his local lord had summoned all of them into service. He was given a horse and a chain mail shirt, and off he went. This was normal; it was just what happened.

They'd ridden for three weeks to get to the battle-field. Slept uneasily that night and then been up since three a.m. to ready themselves for battle that morning.

"Who was the guy?" Jules kept wanting to know. "Who was the guy who showed you the machine?"

"Weird-looking guy, really," said Max, after he'd thought about it for a while. "Kind of like a shop dummy come to life. He was just too clean, too smooth, too per-fect. Neat. He was really neat."

Eventually they got home.

Jules let himself in. Tony was out, so he heated up

some noodles and sat in the dark on the couch. He was starving so he shoveled them down.

Well, this is good, he thought. *I go out to relax and try to forget about everything, and I find there's a JumpMan at my local game parlor, except we can't find it again because the door has disappeared, so I'm probably imagining it all except my friend Max had blood on his hands and knows more about a medieval battle than he could possibly have read in a book. As if Max would ever read.*

Jules walked to the back door before going to bed. He stood on the step and looked out at the night sky.

"Come on, Theo," he said quietly. "Why don't you turn up when I want you to for once."

THE FUTURE
MONDAY LATE AFTERNOON FOURTEEN BILLION AND SEVENTY-THREE

Theo looked down. A long way down. Below him was the coast of Africa. Above him the sky was turning black. He could see the edge of space, the line where there was no more sky, and infinite space began. He was riding a very thin line between existence and oblivion.

He did a few loops. He swooped down past his friends and gave them a chirpy wave. He hummed a little of the last hour's big hit, "I Wanna Really Wanna Gonna Always Wanna" by Sheyney Wheyney.

Sure, he thought, *SolarBlading is spectacular.* There was the curve of the earth. There were the clouds thousands of yards below. There was a sharp stab of the sun around the edge of the planet, and if he looked behind him he could see a mass of stars spread out like spilled diamonds on deep purple velvet. How much more spectacular could anything get?

And sure, he thought, *SolarBlading is fun.* Waiting for a few million tons of hydrogen to explode on the surface of the sun so you could ride a fully charged light wave— how could that not be fun? Hit a sunspot dip or pick up a big solar flare and you could be swooping back down to Earth or spiraling out to the edge of the stratosphere before you knew it. The challenge was to control the blade and ride the light where you wanted to. You also had to watch your speed, because theoretically there was nothing to stop you from SolarBlading at the speed of light. But anyone who'd attempted that had ignited and self-combusted three or four light-seconds later. The trick was to go as fast as you possibly could but not too fast. Otherwise you fried, and that wouldn't be fun.

Theo checked his speed. He yawned, waved at his friends, and peeled off before the solar blast hit them and they all hurtled back toward Earth, screaming with delight, pitching, rolling, somersaulting on the raw light waves of the sun.

Theodore Pine Four was bored. Theodore Pine Four just wasn't into SolarBlading. What Theodore Pine Four was into was TimeJumping.

Theodore headed back home and SolarBladed straight in through his bedroom window. With a flick of his ankles he kicked off his blades. The wall sucked them in and unmade them.

Bored.

"UV reading of 15.8," reported his coat. "Suck, sip, or slurp SunBar. SunBar blocks out harmful rays from the inside. Snap off a SunBar, swallow, and your skin cells will reflect sunlight's harmful UV spectrum. SunBar, next best thing to turning off the sun."

PromoCloth. Free, but the ads never stopped.

Theo was so bored he'd put his HyperCoat on a wall hook and got out his old PromoCloth one. The ads drove him crazy, but now he couldn't even be bothered to turn it off. Maybe it would be interesting to find out how bored you could get. So he left his coat and it kept on going.

"Or, if SunBar's not for you, protect yourself with the Ozone Zone. This small backpack will generate your own personal Ozone Zone that goes where you go. No messy creams, just one hundred percent protection all day long!"

Theo sighed and flopped over on his bed. He stared around his bedroom. One wall was a full color recreation of a supernova. He turned the soundtrack up. Something akin to seven hundred rock bands playing Wagner blasted out from a speaker system so small that it was scattered around his room like dust. He flopped over onto his other side and raised a bored eyebrow. The supernova soundtrack stopped.

"Or don't forget, I'm a coat. If you need me to, I can change to a lightweight long-sleeved top in any one of seven thousand colors or combinations. You'll be protected from the sun's harsh rays—"

"Shut up, coat!" Theo ordered, scratching himself and tossing around on his bed.

He looked around his room again. It was just a normal room. Walls could create anything he needed, or when the weather was pleasant, which was most of the time, they'd roll themselves up and leave the room open to light and air.

"Mirror," he said to the walls, and the wall opposite the supernova became reflective. Theo looked at his hair. He'd been working for a while on a new feature for his own formula of Molecule Follicle Gel, but now he looked at his hair and wondered what else he could possibly do with it that he hadn't done already. He'd been starting to create some extraordinary effects by programming the gel to individually color each strand of hair. This meant that his hair was not just a bright red or yellow, not just a rapidly changing pattern of lightning bolts and swirls and spirals, but something that shimmered and gleamed like light bouncing off a river.

It looked fantastic, but now as he stared at himself in the mirror, he shrugged. His hair was radiating emerald and magenta with an intensity that could be seen from miles away, and he was sick of it. Was that it? Just more and more color? He focused his concentration on his hair, and for a moment it all stood up, and in the front it formed itself into two short devil's horns. A few seconds later the horns collapsed.

Theo sighed. He supposed if he worked at it, he could get the shape-changing function of his gel to do more things, but then what? Wouldn't he get bored with that as he had done with the whole color thing? In the end, a lot of effort and struggle simply to be bored again.

He flopped back on the bed, ordered a window into the wall opposite, and stared out.

Everything looked much as it ever had, but it was

weird how everything had changed. No one wanted to TimeJump anymore. It was over.

Everyone was scared. Oh, they didn't admit they were scared. They all just pretended that SolarBlading was particularly good at the moment, but Theo knew; they weren't thinking about TimeJumping at all. Some kids were even getting out their old Speed-O-Volves and doing some gene-splitting.

Sure, thought Theo, a Speed-O-Volve, some pseudocells, and a packet of instant DNA did give you a pretty hilarious afternoon.

Throw the pseudocells and the DNA into the Speed-O-Volve, set the switch to half a billion years, and who knew what might come out? Purple trees, six-legged armadillos, furry lizards, bananas that talked—they were standard presets on a Speed-O-Volve. Throw any of those back in and program your own climate, predator, habitat decline, and you started to get a show. Your armadillos were nesting in the purple trees, which were the only food for your furry lizard, which was hunted to extinction by a mythical civilization that killed them for their soft downy pelt. And you still had a banana that wouldn't shut up. A lot of kids were saying that it might even be better than TimeJumping.

Not Theo. Theodore Pine Four was a TimeJumper

through and through. All he needed was a JumpMan, and all time was his. He didn't want games or rides, or some machine that spat out garrulous fruit. He wanted to see everything. The whole world and everything that had ever been. He wanted to answer the big questions: How did humans get here? What happened next? Or rather, what happened before, which is the question when you Jump backward through time.

Theo could go anywhere he liked, from the Big Bang till yesterday—just like it said on the box the JumpMan came in. "JumpMan from TimeMaster—maker of JumpMan, JumpMan Pro, and all your TimeJumping accessories. At TimeMaster—We've Always Got Time for You."

Theo loved it. He'd always loved it. And the last few months with Quincy Carter One had turned him completely.

Quincy's tales of the early days when he and Franklin Nixon and the rest of the TimeMaster Six were inventing the process were fantastic. Generally horrific, but fantastic. The early test runs were frightening. There was the time they'd only managed to Jump someone's head back a few hundred years, and they'd had to retrieve it before the rest of the body went into a temporal seizure. Or when they'd Jumped someone back five seconds but were then unable to return him to the present, so he'd stayed five seconds behind for a month. The experiments on SlowTime and FastTime, the disastrous day they'd stopped time. Theo had lapped these stories up.

Even just being back on Earth in those days must have been amazing. The early TimeJumpers were the first to return and establish Earth colonies. No one on Mars was really that interested. They all thought that Earth was over and that there was no reason to bother going back there. Mars was where humans lived now. Earth had been nothing but trouble, and there was nothing to be gained by returning.

Theo had started to feel a deep connection with the tradition of TimeJumping, and it had made it even more special. He'd joined JuniorJumpers as soon as he could, and he'd pretty much been the first in his skwad to do everything; first to do a solo jump, first to do the dozen in a day, first to clock up one thousand sites, but in the last few months it had taken on a whole other level.

He'd become the face of JumpMan after winning a competition to be the first to try out a new model. That had been a disaster, and now it seemed like it was all over. Quincy Carter One, Cheeo of TimeMaster—exposed on Hurrah Banter's ClickDown as a lying, thieving, greedy, power-hungry lunatic, not the cheery eager promoter of JumpMans everyone had thought he was—had disappeared and no one was trusting Time-Jumping anymore. How would we know if the system was safe? Nothing had happened, but who knew if it would stay that way? Quincy might have lain traps, he might come back, he might do anything. Suddenly no one thought TimeJumping was worth the risk.

Their fear was understandable. Anyone who TimeJumped had the TimeCode off by heart, and everyone knew that really it all just came down to one rule and one rule only: Don't Touch Anything. The past is gone, the present never happens, and the future is unknown. You could TimeJump anywhen you liked, so long as there was a JumpSite, but only to look, to observe, and to experience. Not to alter or interact or get involved in any way. If you changed something, there was no way you could know what effect that might have down through the ages.

It was such an important part of Theo's world that when they found that someone was breaking the rule it was bad enough, but then to find out it was Quincy Carter One—the beloved and much admired cheeo of

TimeMaster himself—destroyed everyone's faith in the entire TimeJumping system.

Theo sat up, tuned in his coat, and picked up the weather, which he could pretty much see through the window, but it was interesting to know the exact wind speed and the precise amount of pollen being carried at the moment. He listened to this hour's number two song, "Oooo, Oooo, Oo, Oo, Oooo, OOO" by the luscious AhLee ShaLaSheeLaSholee. He checked his messages and then dumped them all. There were six in a row from friends telling him that the sunspot activity was just wild and he really should come back and blast some rays with them. They'd always been ready to Jump before.

Theo threw his coat at the wall, and the wall made a hook so it hung there.

"Bored, bored, bored," he said, and let himself slide off the bed until his head was resting on the floor. Under the bed, in the far corner, he saw a glint of silver.

It was his old JumpMan. Not the JumpMan Pro he'd won in a Two-Planet competition that had started this whole mess off. Not the JumpMan that Franklin had given him to Jump through time and rescue Genevieve. It was his old faithful standard model JumpMan Sixty.

He reached in and pulled it out. He fumbled about a bit further and found the remote. Both seemed in perfect working order.

He pointed the remote at the JumpMan, and it immediately lifted off the bed and starting hovering at around his head height.

Why not a Jump?

Well, there were some pretty good reasons not to Jump, really. First there was Franklin. One of the original TimeMaster Six, and the only one to suspect Quincy, he'd been adamant. "Don't Jump!" he'd said in the hours after Quincy had vanished and Jules and Gen had returned to Mil 3. "Got it? Don't Jump!" he'd repeated as Theo had opened his mouth to ask why, and to protest Franklin's instruction.

"Why? Why?" screeched Franklin when Theo had finally got past his pointy finger and his constant order not to Jump. "You want to run into Quincy out there somewhere? You want to end up like me, trapped for years in some hellhole? You want to give Quincy the opportunity to find you and hold us all for ransom again? Can I say it any simpler so even an applesticker like you can understand? Don't Jump!"

Franklin had been fairly clear. And that message had gone out to everyone.

No one had cleared any of the Sites, and so JumpSite hit rates were way down. Right now Theo could have TimeJumped to Caesar's Victory Games, featuring gladiators on elephants versus the Ethiopians on tigers, and been the only person there from Fourteen Billion and Seventy-three. And that was one you usually had to book months ahead.

Theo knew no one was Jumping right now. But that didn't mean he couldn't Jump.

He listened out for his mother. She was down the hall, at her desk. His father wouldn't be home until later.

Theo watched his JumpMan spin around his head. He flicked a few buttons on the remote and read the sites coming up on its screen. THREE SECONDS AFTER BIG BANG, ARCHIMEDES AND THE BATH, FORMATION OF THE HIMALAYAS . . .

It was all tempting but perhaps not really worth the risk.

There was one place, however, that was.

One place he'd really love to go.

It didn't have a JumpSite, but Theo figured he knew enough about SiteSearching now to figure it out. So he programmed a wide loose Jump high above the earth's surface, set the time, closed his eyes, and pressed the GoButton.

THE PAST

MIDWINTER EVENING, FULL MOON 13,000 BC OLD TIME

Bug Lover, Two Brow, and Star Speck were inseparable. Which was just as well, because they didn't really have anyone else. By rights they should all have been adults by this time; joining in the hunt, searching for food, having children. But Bug Lover, Two Brow, and Star Speck had always been different. Which is why they were standing now at the bottom of the Meeting Hill, with all of the people of the tribes of the Long River gathered before them.

No other thirteen-year-olds of the tribes of the Long River were calling meetings.

Bug Lover was speaking to them. "Can everyone hear me?" he asked.

No one said anything.

"Ah, yes", said Bug Lover. "Well, I guess if you can't hear me, you're not going to say anything because you can't hear me. Right?"

No response. *Have to think about a way that a crowd can respond all together,* thought Bug Lover. But not now. Time to get on. He'd say his joke.

"Thank you all for coming," he began again. "I know we're all busy. Sometimes by the time I've finished picking up some wheat heads and milking the goat, I've barely got the energy to pull the wife around the cave by her hair."

Silence.

Hmm, he thought. *Saying the opposite of what you mean in order to make the other person do a funny grunt doesn't work for all of them, that's for sure.*

Bug Lover looked out at his crowd. They were all sitting in their tribes, and really they could barely tolerate one another. And right now Bug Lover felt like a member of the smallest tribe there was; the tribe of him and his two friends; they were strange ones that no one else wanted. Look at Star Speck. Well, he kind of looked normal. He was short and dark and muscular. But he was talking almost before he could walk. And then he started counting moons, and before he was ten he could tell you exactly what the moon was going to be and do, and when, and he could read the night sky like the elders could read the clouds.

And Two Brow. Small, delicate. Bug Lover thought she was beautiful, but she was a girl. A tiny little thing no one thought would survive. And here she was hanging around with two males. No one else did that. Still, no one else wanted her. She was as bright as anything, if she'd just get over her obsession with the long-faced beasts, the horses. She'd inherited it, thought Bug Lover, so she didn't have much choice. And what about him? Smart as anything and as twitchy as a rabbit, always hopping from one foot to the other, always ready to run. Annoying habits, but helpful when you were the one everyone else liked to stomp on for sport. He looked up the Meeting Hill. Even that had been his idea. Anyone who needed to speak to the tribes should stand at the bottom of the hill and everyone else should sit on the slope. Everyone could see, everyone could hear.

No turning back, he thought. It was time to get started. Some were already standing up and scratching. A few others had begun to groom one another and eat whatever they found.

"You three up the top, why don't you come down and join us?" he called out.

Three recently arrived hairy people looked blankly down at him. One of them picked his nose and wiped it on himself. His companion licked it off. *Some of these people,* Bug Lover thought. They really should have stayed in the trees. They looked uncomfortable down here on the ground, walking upright.

"All right. Well then, we'll begin anyway."

He drew a deep breath. They were going to love

this. He had a strange feeling about this one. This was the best idea he'd ever had. Everything about it was so right. Every time he looked at it, he saw not just a one-off idea, something that would fix an immediate problem, but something that would change everything forever. He didn't really know how or into what, but he just felt that once they saw this and understood, nothing would ever be the same again.

"First, do we all remember what these groupings are for? We get together, and everyone hears what everyone has to say, as long as they are from a tribe who's learned to speak, and then we can think about it. Remember how we got together and decided that instead of clubbing the women over the head and dragging them off to each other's camps—resulting in a lot of angry women who frankly weren't that great to live with—it might be a lot better if we just asked first and then we could probably figure something out?"

There were some nods and grunts at that, although for the most part the men just stared at him. Bug Lover sighed again. *Must work on showing them that communication requires the other party to communicate as well.*

"So, this is a lot like that. A couple of us here from the rock shelf have come up with something, and we thought we'd show it to you. We want to get everyone involved. This is for all of us. It's not just mine, or just my tribe's. This is for you. You can use it how you like, you can do what you want with it. So . . ."

Bug Lover's mouth went dry. He licked his lips and there was nothing there.

". . . ah, so, why don't I just stop all the talking and let's bring it out, shall we? Star Speck, Two Brow? You want to bring it out now?"

Two figures stepped forward from the shadows. This time there was a reaction from the crowd. Half of them stood up and screamed. Some bared their teeth. At least one threw a spear.

Star Speck and Two Brow weren't carrying anything into the flickering light of the fires. They were rolling it in. It was round. They pushed it a bit more and it rolled in by itself. It stood on its edge for a moment and then flopped over on its side where it lay still.

"I call it a weel!" announced Bug Lover.

chapter two
FROM TIME TO TIME

SiteSearching was simple enough in theory. A JumpSite had to have exact coordinates. In time and in space. You had to know when you were going and where you were going. So you had to start somewhere.

SiteSearchers started with a date. That was easy enough. Pick a time, any time. One hundred years ago. One hundred million years ago. It's all in the past, it's all there. So a SiteSearcher dials up a date.

But where are you going? Is the physical space clear so that a TimeJumper can occupy it? Because you could dial up some space coordinates and if you're not careful there might have been a mountain there, say, one hundred million years ago, and you would then Jump your body's atoms and particles into the side of that mountain. You'd have to stay there. You can't JumpBack if you are now part of a mountain.

You have to check ocean levels, where the continents are, any immediate earthquake activity, let alone if you're Jumping into the immediate past and humans have pushed up a few buildings and laid out some motorways and things. Roads are one of the reasons TimeJumpers don't like Mil 3. Roads everywhere! Trying to find a JumpSite that doesn't have a few tons of truck bearing down on you is almost impossible!

So if you want to locate a Jump site, then your first Jump to a particular time is always set at ten thousand yards above sea level. SiteSearchers literally drop out of the sky. Ten thousand yards above sea level means you won't accidentally impale yourself on Everest.

And again, it's another reason why Mil 3 seems so hostile to TimeJumping. Trying to dodge cruising jumbos when you've just Jumped in is a real pain.

SiteSearchers fall straight down, skydiving without a parachute. The JumpMan takes some pinpoint accurate readings of the surface, and the SiteSearchers Jump themselves back to the sixteenth billennium before they splatter themselves all over the past.

It's wild fun. And as Theo plummeted toward Earth

from the skies above Mil 3, he began to appreciate that it was also something that required training and concentration and a level of experience before doing it on your own. He'd Jumped everywhere, but SiteSearching was something else. Training and experience that Theo hadn't had. This was nothing like SolarBlading, where you had some level of control. This was like falling from a very, very great height.

Theo was screaming. He was sure he was screaming. It felt like he was screaming. He just couldn't hear himself scream.

He was cold. Air was rushing past and through him as he fell hundreds of yards in a few seconds.

His JumpMan, which had hovered quietly by his head in his bedroom, was now just behind him someplace where he couldn't quite see it.

The remote was in his hand, but he couldn't move his arm. He could, but he was so panicked and freaked out by the sensation of falling that he couldn't quite order his brain to move his fingers and his hand as it should.

He kept falling and he kept screaming. Luckily the JumpMan knew what to do. It moved out from behind his head and came to hover just by his ear.

Theo summoned all the concentration he could, and

at around the moment when he could start to see that what a few seconds ago had been a collection of tiny buildings far below him was now a quite large city, and he could see the roads and the cars, he managed to press the GoButton and Jump himself back into his bedroom.

He was still screaming even as he stood there looking out the window at the world of Fourteen Billion and Seventy-three. His mother came up on the wall where the spectacular picture of a supernova had been. He stopped.

"Theo?" she said. "Was that you screaming? Is that a JumpMan? What are you doing in there?"

"Mam!" said Theo in a deeply wounded tone. "You promised not to FlopScreen me! Didn't you see the sign? Can't you read?"

"When you are screaming in your bedroom, young man, I ignore your acute sense of privacy and come in to see if you're all right. Now, put that JumpMan down. You know what the United Planets are saying. It's not safe."

Theo was reminded for a moment of his recent plummeting trip toward Earth and thought she might be right. But he wasn't going to let that worry him.

Time for a distraction. He let the JumpMan settle on the bed and then moved himself in front of it.

"Dud home?" he asked.

"Not yet," said his mam. "Things are so crazy, I don't expect him for a while."

Theo nodded.

"You'll get wallfood if you're hungry, Oak-I?"

"Yip, Mam," said Theo.

His mam disappeared and the supernova returned, a black hole sucking in stars near the top like a kid slurping up a ValarShake.

Theo looked at his JumpMan. He read the readout on the screen of the remote. He had some coordinates. Might as well try again.

It took him ten goes to get it figured out, but within about an hour he had a JumpSite fixed, and he was wandering in through the gates of Rosemount High.

He was, as had always been the case until the recent aberrations, about ten nanoseconds behind local time. He was therefore not "present" and was invisible to the locals. He didn't want to disturb anything. He just wanted to see how Jules and Gen were. And, despite the way most people of his time felt about Mil 3, Theo had started to like it. It was funny. And one of the places he'd most enjoyed was Rosemount High.

Everywhere he looked, it was funny.

Take these kids, he thought. *They all look like turtles. They've got backpacks on that are as big as they are. What are they carrying around? Why not just call up any book or bit of info you want on a computer? What's with the big heavy books? And then they've got sports clothes, and lunches and raincoats, and all sorts of other junk in there, and they seem to have to lug them everywhere they go.*

Theo walked around, smiling at the clothes and the hairstyles. There were kids with streaks and highlights, and some kids were shaved and others were purple all over. Theo fired up his own using his Molecule Follicle Gel and made it a deep rich brown with creamy spots and swoops, like a chocolate dessert. He would have loved to just grab some of them and show them a thing or two about styling, but this time he was going to have to be content with watching for a bit.

Maybe he should start doing some JumpTours here? He could open up a Site. Kids would love this. And then he remembered that kids weren't loving TimeJumping at all, and trying to convince them that a Mil 3 school would be a fascinating Site might be a bit hard.

But wouldn't they be as intrigued as he was? For example, what was wrong with the classrooms? They didn't work at all.

The kids went in, sat down, and immediately fell quiet, looked bored, and all but shut down completely. Only three of the kids there would put their hands up to answer anything; everyone else tried to avoid any eye contact or interaction with the teacher. None of them talked to anyone else except in guarded little mutterings out of the corner of their mouths. If the teacher tried to involve someone other than the three kids who always put their hands up, nothing happened. The kid selected just shrugged and mumbled a bit, waiting for the teacher to give up and move on.

But then as soon as the bell went, this pack of worn-out and weary looking prisoners, who'd been sighing and yawning and responding with all the energy of slugs in the sun, came out into the corridors and suddenly burst into vibrant activity. They rushed around, found each other, collided and bounced off one another like overcharged electrons. They started yelling and chatting away at an incredible rate. They revealed deep understanding and an astonishing amount of knowledge about games and wizards and other galaxies. They showed an intimate understanding of one another's character and personality and history as they minutely analyzed everything that was going on around them.

Should teach the classes out in the corridor, thought Theo.

Theo found the whole process fascinating. In his time he spent his day in a learning session. He learned things from his coat, from his FlopScreen, and occasionally he got together with his mentor and four other kids and did some stuff, but that was about it. It just didn't give rise to the same kind of gossip you get from thirty kids in a class, a hundred in a year, and six or seven hundred in a school. The mere fact that they brought seven hundred or so kids together and let them interact like this, he thought, was totally radical.

As far as Theo could gather, there was a whole life going on that none of the teachers or adults knew anything about at all. This was the real life of the school, and in his time it just wouldn't be allowed. So Theo walked up and down the halls, in and out of classrooms, watching kids fight, play, talk, get together, break up, get together, and break up again. He loved following them and eavesdropping on a conversation so deep or a confidence so important that everything else faded into the background. Or he loved to hang out on the edge of a group of five or six, trying to pick up on the rhythm of the conversation, and enjoying the happy vibe that only a group of friends can generate.

Sometimes at lunchtime or after school he liked to sit where he could see the whole yard, and watch everyone flow around the place. From that point he would try to pick up the rules that were never stated, the laws and customs that everyone but he understood.

Really, a Mil 3 school, thought Theo, much to his own surprise, was everything you wanted from a Jump site, and he wished he could either share it with some of his own friends or at least go and hang out with Jules and Gen. The truth was, he really missed them.

Theo left the yard and walked back into the school. He'd do one more round and then JumpBack home. As he came in through the front doors, there was Jules coming toward him.

Theo stepped off to one side, and smiled a little. He'd come to like Jules. And really, he had to admit that in the Jumps they'd done together, it had been Jules who had done the real work.

Hip, that's not right, he thought. *He looks unhappy. What's wrong with him?*

Jules drew level and stopped. Then his head whipped around and looked straight at Theo. Jules frowned, looked even more upset, and walked on.

Phip, that was close, thought Theo. *Did he see me? How could he have?*

Theo checked again. He was invisible. But it definitely felt like Jules had been looking straight at him for a second or two. He'd seemed to stop right where Theo was.

His coat started ringing. Who'd be calling him there?

A small screen popped out from the lapel of his coat. A skinny, sharp-looking face with a bony nose and piercing gaze appeared.

"Theo. Let me think. . . . Did I say, 'Don't Jump'?"

"Franklin!" said Theo, trying hard to sound pleased to see him.

"Don't even pretend. Get back here. Now!"

The screen went black and then came on again.

"And come to MeanTime."

MeanTime? wondered Theo as he checked his presets on his JumpMan.

There it was, MeanTime. The number one preset. The emergency Jump if all else failed.

No one ever used it. So why would Franklin want him to go there?

Only one way to find out. Theo Jumped.

THE PRESENT
MONDAY MORNING EARLY MIL 3

When Gen came out her front door to head to school, there was a familiar shape slumped against the fence.

"Jules!" she called. *He's come to walk me to school,* she thought. *Nice way to start the week.*

"How are you, cool guy?" she asked.

"Don't," he said as they walked off together.

"Don't what?"

"The 'cool guy' thing. It's freaking me out."

"Why? It's funny."

"Doesn't it just tell you that everything is wrong?"

"No."

"No? You get kidnapped and trapped in Pompeii. You nearly die. We find out that Quincy wants to kill us. The entire school and all of our parents get TimeSwept so they won't remember any of the action, and all of them have been completely weird ever since. You seriously don't think everything is wrong?"

The last TimeJump had really unsettled Jules. Not the Jump itself, but everything since. Until the first Monday after the weekend when there'd been two weekends, in the order of coolness at Rosemount High, Jules had been somewhere near the bottom. He wasn't the most uncool kid at Rosemount High—that was Dean, who'd walked in holding hands with his mother at the last parent-teacher night—but Jules was still something of a new kid. Nothing he did was cool, he owned nothing cool, the cool people were not his friends.

Jules, nearly fourteen, a guy who knew he was pretty much average in every respect, a guy who usually dragged himself into Rosemount High with all the enthusiasm of a dog checking itself into the pound, was now getting the kind of recognition only given to someone who is officially cool.

Take the four-headed monster, for example. Gen and her three best friends, Sonja, Kyeela, and Bonnie, who formed a single organism that survived on gossip, real and imagined, had always regarded him as a kind of virus. When she was with them, even Gen tended to pretend like he was something to be wiped up and disposed of.

But when he arrived at school now, they waved at him. They called him over, they spoke to him. The first time it happened, Jules had even looked behind to see who they were waving at, done a double take when he realized it was him, pointed at his chest and said, "Me?" before looking around again, just to make sure.

He'd walked over and Sonja had said, "Hi, Jules," and then squeezed his arm. Squeezed his arm.

Jules had stared back at her. "Hi," he'd managed eventually.

Kyeela had smiled at him. "What did you do on the weekend, Jules?"

She had never wanted to know what he'd done on the weekend. No one had ever wanted to know what he'd done on the weekend.

"Ah, nothing much."

"Yeah right, you always say that and then it always turns out you were doing something amazing!"

What?

What? his brain joined in. *I'm sorry, I usually run off when these girls turn up. They're so annoying. But are they really being friendly? And did she just say you usually do amazing things?*

I think so.

Jules was so shocked he forgot he didn't want to talk to his brain anymore. He was so shocked that he barely said anything for the five minutes he stood there while the girls laughed and chatted at him. The girls who'd always treated him as though he were so low on the radar that he wasn't even flying, were now turning their full spotlight smiles on him, and even though all he was saying was "Yeah" and "Huh?" they were listening to him as though all of a sudden he were witty and wise. He sort of liked it, but he certainly didn't trust it.

Jules was sure that just as he was getting used to it and starting to enjoy it, the girls would turn around and there would be the old sneers, the usual snubs, the eye-rolling, the impatient flicks of the hair, the just-don't-even-bother-to-look-at-me looks.

But it hadn't stopped. And even though Jules had

seen a Minotaur and a whole host of other weird things in recent months, there was nothing more unsettling to him than to get up each morning, go to school, and be seen as cool.

What had happened to everyone? Was he at the right school? Was this an elaborate joke that everyone was in on?

He went to the bathroom and took a good hard look at himself in the mirror. No, he wasn't Keanu Reeves, or Brad Pitt. He was still Jules Santorini, kind of ordinary-looking, not so fair, not so foul, but kind of in the middle.

This was very strange. And after a few days of it, he was edgy.

"It doesn't worry you?" he said to Gen as they waited at the traffic lights.

"Yeah. A bit," replied Gen.

"A bit? Everything's mad, and you're worried *a bit*?"

"Yeah, okay, Jules."

Gen looked away, and walked off ahead of him as soon as the lights turned green. She didn't want him to see the biting tears that had sprung into her eyes.

"What?" he squawked, running to catch up to her.

"Slow down," he demanded, grabbing her by the arm.

"Leave me alone, Jules!" Gen pulled her arm away.

And then stood still, her shoulders slumping.

Jules stood behind her.

Good one.

What do I do?

Oh, need me, do you?

A little. What do you do when girls cry?

You wait for a minute. And then you say you're sorry.

Jules waited a moment.

"Sorry, Gen," he mumbled. "I don't know what's wrong with me."

"Well, could you shut up for a while? How do you think I feel?"

"Yeah, sorry. I don't know. How do you feel?"

She swung around to face him. "I'm really scared, Jules. I can still smell the gas, and my throat's still burned. I got away. Everyone else . . ."

Jules looked around awkwardly, hoping there were no other kids coming this way to school. There were. He jerked a head in their direction, and they both started walking again.

He felt better. Not because he had made Gen cry, but because at least she was scared as well. It wasn't just him.

"Your parents weird?" asked Jules, thinking about his own dad who, since the last Jump, had started to stop Jules three times a day and tell him he loved him. It was kind of good, but once a year would have been enough.

Gen nodded.

"They're being so nice. I've got new clothes. I'm back in my room. Cynthia's back in hers. And look at this."

Gen pulled a small flat object from her pocket. It was slim, and curved a little along the sides. It had a swirling pink cover, and a small LCD screen at one end. In her hand Gen held the single most desirable item for any girl with the word "teen" in her age.

"They got you a phone?" said Jules.

Gen nodded. "Can you believe it?"

Gen flicked a couple of numbers with her thumb. She made a huge effort to try to look like she did this all the time, like she was someone who was always checking her messages and texting friends, but she was just too pleased with it and kept grinning and spinning around. She stopped and turned to Jules.

"Wait till the girls all get one. That'll be fantastic."

She grinned again and looked at Jules's tight face.

"Jules, it's hard, right? But you're not helping me. Every time I see you, all you want to talk about is Theo and Quincy."

"Well, hell, Gen. The most powerful man in the future wants to kill us. Us. You and me. Why?"

"I don't know, Jules! Apparently we're going to grow

up and do something that he doesn't want us to do. And if I think about it anymore, I'm going to go mad."

Gen ran off into the school.

"There's a JumpMan at Blast!" he yelled at Gen's retreating back.

Gen stopped. She turned around and looked at him with a kind of pitying look.

"You've been going to Blast?"

"I only went once. There's a JumpMan."

"You saw it?"

"No. Max did."

"Oh, Max. Well, now I believe it."

"No, he did. He described it. He Jumped."

Jules had walked up to join her. She put a hand on his shoulder. "You need to calm down, Jules. Relax."

She leaned forward, brushed his cheek with her lips, and walked off into school, ignoring the whoops and jeers of a group of boys who had noticed she'd been kissing Jules.

That wasn't much of a kiss, you know, said his brain.

It was okay.

Okay? A kiss shouldn't be okay. A kiss should be—

Brain. I don't think I want to talk to you anymore.

You keep saying that.

I keep meaning it too.

Don't be like that, Jules. We've always got on so well.

Don't you think it's time I stopped talking to my brain?

Why?

I'm nearly fourteen; I can't be talking to you. I may as well have an imaginary friend.

Nothing imaginary about me. I'm your brain. Most complex thing so far discovered in the universe. Capable of making billions of calculations and connections every single second. I can chew gum and make your heart beat at the same time. I—

Yes, I know. But other people don't talk to their brains. I don't want to anymore either.

How do you know?

Know what?

How do you know other people don't talk to their brains? Does anyone know you do?

No.

Well, how do you know other people don't?

They just don't, okay?

I'll let you in on a secret. They do.

Jules tried desperately to slam the door shut on his brain. He'd been talking to his brain for years, so it wasn't an easy habit to break. He walked into school, and despite what Gen had said, his mind went back to thinking about Quincy. Quincy Carter One, rich, powerful, ruthless, and mad. Was he still looking for them? Could he come and get them anytime? Why not? He could Jump in, and then Jump him and Gen off to a nice empty part of the past. Somewhere a billion years ago with a lot of hot mud, sulphurous smoke, and a few half-evolved salamanders for company. Somewhere and somewhen no one would ever find.

"Hey, Jules!"

Someone was calling out to him.

"Jules! We've got the first class together. Let's go, man."

"Man?"

Someone called him "man"?

Jules looked around to see if anyone else was called Jules or Man, but no, there was some kid calling out to him, and everyone else nodding respectfully at him and saying "Jules" and "Yo" and "All right" at him.

What had happened? Had Earth shifted a little on its axis and the magnetic forces were now affecting everyone's brain? Was there a bacteria eating everyone's brain?

Jules wasn't used to this much attention. He backed away and pretended to be looking through his locker.

He needed to think.

Come on, why don't you just lie back and enjoy it? his brain urged.

Go away! You never help me! You're just another weird thing in an entire world of weird things.

And then there was the one question that no one had been able to answer. Why was Quincy so interested in them? What were he and Gen going to do that would interest someone who lived 3,000 years in the future?

His mother had said he needed to free his mind, and right now he wanted to be gazing out over a vast still ocean, or looking up into an infinite sky, anything that might calm him down a little. And then just as he began to imagine the ocean, transporting himself far away from the noisy school, he saw him. Only for a second, and only at the very edge of his vision, but Jules was sure it was him.

Theo.

Theo?

And that was about how long it took. As soon as Jules stopped and looked at him directly, he wasn't there.

Great, thought Jules, breathing out a long deep frustrated sigh and slumping back onto his locker. *Great. I'm cool, and now I'm officially going mad. I'm hallucinating and going mad and everyone's watching me. Excellent.*

Jules turned around, banged his head a few times on the locker, and then headed off to class. Maybe there he could find some peace for a moment or two.

THE PAST

MIDWINTER EVENING, FULL MOON 13,000 BC OLD TIME

Bug Lover stood up with his hands out. The crowd erupted as the weel rolled across the grass in front of them, rolled in a few smaller circles, and then fell over.

"Please! Quiet! It's all right!" he shouted, but he couldn't be heard. One tribe had started a battle plan. Another was yelling to its gods in the ground. The three up at the top of the hill had started screaming over and over again. But Bug Lover saw as he tried to quiet them down that Moon Smacked had got up with a puzzled look on his face and gone over to the weel and was now poking at it with his feet. Star Speck and Two Brow looked at Bug Lover, unsure of what to do.

Oh well, thought Bug Lover, *it's going to be one of those ideas—one person at a time.* So ignoring the crowd for a moment, he went over to Moon Smacked. Keeping his eyes on him, he bent down and picked up the weel.

"It's all right," he said. "It can't hurt you."

"What did you say you call this thing?" asked Moon Smacked.

"A weel," said Bug Lover.

"Weel. Weel. Weel," tried Moon Smacked. "I think it should be more like wheel."

"Wheel? Wheel," tried Bug Lover. Frankly, he couldn't really tell the difference, but if it would make Moon Smacked happy and get him onside . . .

"All right. Wheel, it is. Thanks, Moon Smacked."

Moon Smacked nodded as though he'd done something really important, and then poked at the wheel a bit more with his foot.

"Um, if I may?" offered Bug Lover. "You pick the wheel up and put it on its side. And then you give it a little push and off it goes."

The wheel rolled back along the grass to the other side, where Two Brow and Star Speck watched nervously. The crowd stopped screaming and fighting and planning and watched it again. It bounced over a rock or two and then slowed down and fell over.

Moon Smacked nodded and put on his serious look. "I see," he said. "So this wheel, that's what it does?"

"That's what it does!" said Bug Lover happily. "Isn't it amazing? One little push and it goes all the way over there."

"One little push," said Moon Smacked.

"That's right. One little push."

"And we could go over there now and give it one little push and it would roll back again?"

"We could do that, we could roll it anywhere we like."

"Just keep on rolling it?"

"Two Brow rolled it once from just after we'd eaten some dried crickets for breakfast until the sun was high in the sky!"

"That long?"

"Uh-huh," said Bug Lover, astonished that Moon Smacked was the one who seemed to be grasping it and all of its potential. He noticed also that the crowd was starting to quiet down a little, and a few more had come over to listen to Bug Lover and Moon Smacked talk about it.

"How do you make one?" a tall lanky Red Tree tribesman asked.

"You need a lot of very sharp cutting rocks. You take a rolling log and chop off one end, make it about as thick as your arm, and there's your wheel."

"You chopped up a rolling log?"

"Well, only a little—"

"A perfectly good rolling log?"

"One that was nearly—"

"You ruin a good rolling log to make this?"

The lanky one was not that impressed with the whole thing after all. He sniffed at the wheel and then in a deeply insulting gesture he squatted over it and lifted up his bearskin.

If Bug Lover had been a little bigger, he would have challenged this deeply insulting gesture by hurling rocks at the lanky one's head, but as Bug Lover was not much bigger than a child, he had no choice but to laugh a little nervous laugh, wave, and say, "All right, all right. You'll see. It's going to be really very good."

Bug Lover felt the knots and nerve-jangling in his stomach intensify. The groups were settling down again, and watching as Moon Smacked continued to push and poke at the wheel. He seemed to be doing the running for all of them.

"Can I do it?" asked Moon Smacked.

"Please!" said Bug Lover.

Moon Smacked picked up the wheel, balanced it on its side, and gave it a little push, and it rolled all the way over to the other side, struck a rock, turned, and then rolled in ever-decreasing circles until it fell over.

Bug Lover grinned at Two Brow and Star Speck.

"What do you do with it?"

Bug Lover's grin faded a little. Moon Smacked was standing right in front of him, his breath smelling like something had died in his throat about two weeks ago. Bug Lover could see the grit on his large lower lip and the cunning look in Moon Smacked's big sunken eyes. Moon Smacked had been setting Bug

Lover up, and now he was closing in for the kill.

"Do with it?" echoed Bug Lover.

"What do you do with it?" Moon Smacked repeated.

"I'm—I'm—We—I'm—Well, can't you see? It rolls! On its own. Rolling logs don't do that. You have to keep pushing them. The wheel—it rolls!"

"Yes. But what do you do with it?" Moon Smacked hadn't stopped staring at Bug Lover. The place had gone silent. This was a very interesting question. What would you do with it?

Bug Lover was stumped. He'd been so excited when he'd thought of it. He'd been walking by as the log rollers were moving a woolly mammoth carcass into a cave. Hog Man, one of his least favorite fellow primates, had picked up a branch and whacked him over the head with it as he'd walked past. That was Hog Man being affectionate. Bug Lover had been knocked out and had fallen to the ground. Thus he'd been lying on his front with his face turned sideways and half-buried in the mud when the log rollers had come by.

Log rolling was quite clever, really. Log rollers found as many smooth round logs as they could and then put them all together. Give a push at the back and all the logs roll forward. Put something heavy on top and you could roll it toward your destination. All the log rollers had to do was take the log at the back and bring it around to the front. A good log-rolling team could move a dead mammoth over quite a lot of land in just a few days. As Bug Lover had come back to consciousness, the log rollers had been just going by, and so Bug Lover had been staring at the ends of the logs. He'd had a sudden vision. Why use the whole log? Why not just the end of the log?

He'd sat straight up, pulling his face out of the mud and barely noticing the bump on the back of his head and the pounding headache starting up. He'd run back to his village and grabbed Two Brow and Star Speck.

"Know where we can get an old rolling log?" he'd asked slyly.

They'd snuck one out of the rolling-log yard and set to work with the sharpest tools they could find. By sunset they had it. A circle of wood, about as high as Bug Lover's knee, that rolled when you pushed it.

Bug Lover had fallen asleep that night with a head full of visions, none of which he could quite understand. He felt like this rolling weel, as he called it, was just so exciting that everyone else would see his excitement and understand it, and that he wouldn't have to do anything but unveil it.

"So, what do you do with it?" Moon Smacked was still asking.

"I don't know," Bug Lover said eventually in a quiet voice.

Moon Smacked turned away with a smirk. The other tribes hated Bug Lover's tribe. They didn't go away on the hunt. They didn't dig deep into the mud for roots and beetles. They stayed around the village like women, building shelters, tending to what they called crops, and looking after some goats. And for that the tribes were meant to give them food. And for some reason, Bug Lover's tribe always seemed to have plenty of food, always seemed healthy, seemed to work half as much as everyone else, and even seemed to have some food left over to put away for the winter, or to trade with others for some nice bearskins. And as much as they'd have preferred not to, the hunters and the gatherers had to use the Tribe That Cannot Hunt or their houses fell down and their goats got sick and their crops came up full of weeds.

Making Bug Lover look stupid was very satisfying to Moon Smacked, who was soon the center of an admiring crowd. They all retired to a favorite rock shelf, leaned on it, and started to drink rotting root juice. They repeated the story to each other over and over, and every time they got to Moon Smacked's asking "What do you do with it?" they broke out into raucous crowing.

Bug Lover huddled down in his scrape. All night he could hear Moon Smacked and his friends drinking and yelling. The story seemed to get longer and Moon Smacked's role bigger as the night went on. Well, he'd show them. He just had to untangle these dreams he kept having and see what was in them. Then he'd sort out what the wheel was for.

A little before dawn everyone went home. Back to their caves, their hollow logs, and their mud shelters. All was quiet. Only Bug Lover was awake, lying in the dirt, looking up at the stars.

THE FUTURE
WEDNESDAY LATE AFTERNOON FOURTEEN BILLION AND SEVENTY-THREE

Theo opened his eyes. He was standing on a hill high above the surrounding countryside. He could see for miles around. In front of him there was a river winding away in the middle distance, and it was surrounded by the ruins of an ancient city. The ruins spread away as far as the horizon. Some crumbling tall towers in front of him, a bridge or two, and then miles and miles of deserted streets and run-down suburbs where once there must have been functioning houses and millions of people.

Alongside him were three or four ramshackle old buildings that might have been sheds or stables. On the corner of one of them was an odd-looking tower with a ball on top of it.

Franklin was leaning against a rusty gate, waiting for him. He straightened up as Theo approached.

"Hi," said Theo. "Nice to see you again, Franklin—oww!"

Franklin had grabbed him by the ear.

"You like the London Jumps, don't you?" he asked.

"Oww!" moaned Theo.

"Don't you?" asked Franklin again, pinching Theo's ear a little harder.

"Yip! Oww! What are you doing?"

"Oh, you seem to enjoy real history so much I thought I'd give you some right now. This is what an old-fashioned English schoolmaster in about 1822 Old Time might have done. Grabbed a naughty boy by the ear and hauled him up to the front for a good caning. Would you like a good caning, Theo?"

"Nip! Oww, stop! What's a caning?"

"Never mind. Did I tell you not to Jump?"

Franklin was dragging Theo by the ear through the gate and into one of the buildings.

"Did I?" Franklin twisted Theo's ear a little.

"Yip! Nip! Oak-I, you told me not to, so what?"

"So what? So what if someone else apart from me and Duncan had picked up where you were going? What if they'd closed down TimeJumping while you were out there? What if I tell you to do something, and you don't do it?"

Franklin tossed Theo by the ear through a doorway.

Theo felt hot prickles of tears behind his eyes.

"What's got into you, Franklin? I just did a little Jump. I wanted to—"

Theo stopped, feeling a little embarrassed.

"Yip?" said Franklin slowly. "What did you want?"

"I just wanted to see Jules and Gen again. Make sure they were all right."

Franklin brought his face up close to Theo's. "That's nice. But very stupid. It's not over. Quincy's out there."

Franklin stood up and swirled down the corridor into a room crammed full of meters, dials, readouts, FlopScreens, and clocks. Clocks were everywhere. Rows and rows of little digital ones, banks of round clean-faced traditional ones. Along the ceiling were yet more rows of tiny digital readouts and round clocks. Each had a code underneath indicating place, era, zone, and any other information that you might need if you were the TimeKeeper.

Sitting in the room was a very good-looking young man who darted from his stool as they came in. "What's that?" he said, peering at a screen. "What's happening to the can opener?"

Franklin stopped and looked puzzled. "Duncan?" he asked. "Is that you, Duncan?"

"Franklin," said the young man, turning to him. "Trust you to look your age."

"Duncan?" It was the first time that Theo had ever seen Franklin really confused. "But, Duncan, you look about twelve."

"Oh come on, Franklin, I look exactly twenty-eight. My favorite age. Remember when we were twenty-eight? I'd just found the Big Bang; I was hotter than helium! We were huge then. So why not? Quick trip to Mars, bought some new skin, had my eyes replaced, got the voice transplant—I feel fantastic!"

Theo agreed. He did look pretty good. Franklin, however, was his usual wrinkled and crabby self.

"Yip, well, try being in Egypt with the pharaohs for the last forty years. Not so good for the looks."

"Franklin, get some ReGen when you're next on Mars. Believe me, I know what time can do to us. I'm the TimeKeeper, right?"

Even Franklin was a little dazzled by Duncan's perfect

smile. He remembered him as a small man, somewhat shy, but now his old friend, who must have been over one hundred, looked like a sprightly young man in the full bloom of youth. He looked way too young to have been one of the original TimeMaster Six, the discoverer of the precise location in space and time of the Big Bang, and now the TimeKeeper, in charge of all time.

"You brought the Pest," observed Duncan.

"The Pest? Him?" replied Franklin. "You mean Theo?"

"The Pest has a name? Theo. You were more trouble than a dropped minute!"

Duncan walked over to Theo. Duncan was shortish, but he seemed to tower over Theo.

Duncan shook his head ruefully. "Day you won that new JumpMan? Nothing's gone right since."

"I'm sorry, Duncan. It wasn't really my fault. I—"

"Yip, I know," he said with a sudden friendly smile. "But when you're trying to keep track of all time, and balance time lost from time found, keeping track of wasted time, and time that's been killed altogether, I don't really need someone bouncing around Mil 3 all on their own."

"Well, that was because—"

"Oh, I know, I know. And look, if I had my way you wouldn't be anywhere—"

"You've got him started now," muttered Franklin. "Duncan, let's just look at what's going on."

But Duncan was firing off on his favorite topic. "A JumpMan is not a toy! It's not just there to amuse you. It was to recover the past. We didn't know Earth anymore. We didn't know where we'd come from. It was Quincy who took this exquisite instrument and turned it into something for kids!" Duncan snorted. "You think we did all that work so a bunch of bored kids'd have something to do on a Saturday?"

"Duncan, we've got some work to do."

But Duncan wasn't about to be interrupted.

"Time! People go on like there's no end to time. But there is. People think they can just Jump anywhere and not tell anyone about it. And then if their particles start drifting off, who's meant to keep track of it, hmm?"

He was going on as if he'd had no one to talk to for a long time.

He fixed his gaze on Theo, and Theo cowered a little.

"I don't think we should be TimeJumping at all! They're still not here, you know?"

Franklin groaned. "Oh, not this, Duncan. I go away for forty years and you're still going on about exactly the same stuff!"

Duncan whirled around to face Franklin.

"Because they're still not here!" Duncan had a wild look in his eyes now. "Where are the TimeJumpers of the future? Why don't they Jump in to check us out? They don't, you know. I'd know if they did. And they don't."

Duncan lowered his voice, widened his eyes, and looked around in case there was anyone lurking in dark corners.

"Something very bad is going to happen." He nodded grimly.

Theo wasn't sure how to respond to all this. It wasn't even very clear what Duncan was talking about, but thankfully Franklin stepped in.

"Duncan's always assumed that there was actually no point inventing TimeJumping. Why not wait until someone invents it in the future? Then they could Jump in and give it to us."

Theo looked a bit puzzled at that one.

"If TimeJumping is successful, then our children will have it, and their children, and so on. So someone from the future must come and visit us at some point. The fact that they haven't just proves it can't be done. So why bother trying?"

"What about Rule One?" asked Theo. "Maybe they're here now but just looking. We can't see them."

"Good point!" said Duncan. "Not bad for a pest. But in the thousands of years to come—not one? Not one little visitor from the future? Not one hint? Not even someone dropping by to say thank you? Or even to tell us not to?"

Duncan was warming up now. "That's right," he said. "It was a great disappointment to me when Franklin and Quincy finally got it worked out. I've regretted it ever since."

"But unless someone invents it," said Theo, "no one in the future will have it, so they can't Jump back and visit you."

"But it's obvious we fail because no one has ever come back."

"But you only fail up until the moment you invent it."

"But if we had invented it—"

"Sorry to butt in," said Franklin pleasantly. "We have to catch up at some stage and I know you love this discussion, but we do have a few problems to deal with. Remember? That's why we're here? Hmm, Duncan?"

Duncan kept staring at Theo for a few seconds longer, and then he tore his gaze away to stare at Franklin.

"Yip," he said. "Oak-I, well, TimeJumping's been officially suspended. United Planets want me to close all

JumpSites right now. You think we can stall them? I close them, we could leave Quincy out there and have no way of getting to him. And I've got a time ripple. Can opener's disappeared. How am I meant to fix that?"

Theo couldn't believe what he was hearing.

"What? They—They want to do what?" he stammered.

"They want to close it down," said Franklin. "The entire system. The only solution, they say, is to leave Quincy out there whenever he may be and close down TimeJumping forever." Franklin shrugged. "There've always been people who didn't like TimeJumping, you know. There've always been people who thought that this is exactly what might happen. It's happened once. What if Quincy tries again? What was that about the can opener?"

"Yip. The can opener has unhappened. It's meant to be invented there, but it hasn't been. See, the can is still invented back here, and thirty years later someone figured out how to open it. Now something's made it unhappen. I'm tracing it, but it'll take a while."

Theo still couldn't believe what he was hearing. "They've banned TimeJumping?"

"It's true," said Duncan. "Take a look. News!" he barked at a FlopScreen.

Up on the screen came an animated computer figure, a reader. It was programmed to read the news exactly as it needed to be read, and to look exactly as each viewer would like their reader to look. Duncan's was a prim-looking woman in glasses with thick wavy hair and just a hint of lipstick.

"Tiny touches of pastel pink on short socks are this hour's hottest fashion, and are there limits to ReGening? Studies show that more than one head transplant in a year may cause complications. Those stories and more later, but first, the end is in sight for TimeMaster. Once the biggest company on the Two Planets, its cheeo, Quincy Carter, is still at large somewhere in the last fourteen billion years. Following the official suspension of TimeJumping and talk of closing the Jump sites entirely, it seems like the end is near."

Theo stared at the FlopScreen as it filled up with option tiles. He could have chosen to hear the official announcement, or a history of Quincy, or even a story about himself and what had happened since he won the JumpMan Pro competition, but he was too shocked to choose. He let the cover story roll: "Until a full investigation into whatever Quincy Carter was doing at all relevant JumpSites can be made, no one should Time-Jump for any reason whatsoever," the reader said.

The screen filled with option tiles again.

"This is only confirming what has already been going on. Jump rates are way down, to levels not seen since the time-freeze scare of Fourteen Billion and Sixty-two. In other news, Martian researchers say they could ReGene cats but make them much nicer—"

Franklin rolled up the FlopScreen and threw it on a bench.

"Ha! You're the last TimeJumper, Theo! It's over. No one wants to know. Once a United Planets sub-bunch get onto it, it could be years before anything happens."

"Nip!" Theo was reeling from all of this. "Franklin, this is all wrong! This is just what a pack of aquatofu-munching Martian rentheads think. What about us?"

Franklin's crinkled face showed a hint of a smile. Theo had the Earthborn's passion for TimeJumping. When Theo Jumped, he saw the history of his own planet. When Martians Jumped they saw funny old-fashioned people grubbing in the dirt to survive. Theo had known only Earth, was proud to be an Earthborn, and didn't see Earth as the Martians saw it. They thought it was backward, dirty, and that it should be left to the armadillos and whatever else had survived. Theo thought it was beautiful and amazing, and he couldn't understand why the Martians were so dismissive of it.

"Nip! There's got to be something we can do, Franklin."

Franklin stuck a tongue in his cheek and then rolled it around his teeth.

"Oak-I," he said. "You want to go Jumping, right?"

Theo nodded.

"All right. Well, maybe we should use that. Here's what we're going to do. Duncan's going to be monitoring and holding time in place. The JumpSystem's still there, but we're really the only three who have access to it. I want you to start to Jump in and out of Sites and report back on anything that shouldn't be happening. We'll pick it up here, but you may be able to get a better handle being on the Site itself."

Franklin handed him a printout of JumpSites.

"Begin with these, and we'll look for any hint of when Quincy might be. I'll start thinking about what to tell them on Mars."

Franklin scowled at Theo and made a little sweeping motion with his hand. "Off you go. Start Jumping."

So Theo Jumped.

He checked that Tutankhamen was still a boy king and about to have a fabulous funeral. He counted Henry VIII's wives. He made sure Charles Darwin was still poking about the Galapagos Islands. He watched Archimedes run a bath.

And in between he popped into Mil 3. No one told him not to. Not this time, anyway. And he thought he really should warn Jules and Gen about what was going on. Things were hotting up and whenever they did, it usually involved them as well.

He sat in class next to Jules, invisible and quiet. *I should talk to him,* he thought. But he couldn't do it there. Jules'd freak out and the whole thing would be a mess.

How to get him to stay back a little so he could talk to him alone?

The class ended. The kids exploded toward the door. Jules pulled his attention in from the window and gathered up his things.

Theo started writing on the blackboard. He finished his message, turned around, and saw Jules's white face.

His coat screamed at him. It was Franklin.

"Sorry, Jules, gotta go. Talk to you soon."

And he Jumped.

chapter three
TIME BOMB

THE PRESENT

MONDAY MORNING EARLY MIL 3

Jules came out of class.

He turned around and watched everything around him slow down. The crowd of kids coming and going from other rooms swirled by him in slow motion, some nodding and waving and calling out his name. They sounded like humpback whales singing.

He stumbled his way along the wall until he reached the bathroom. He went in, found a booth, and sat down, head slumped in his hands, and had a huge fight with his brain.

Brain! Did you see that?

I thought you didn't want to talk to me.

I don't. But did you see that?

I don't have eyes, as such, Jules. What did you see?

Theo. Did you see Theo?

I don't "see." I collect data from your retina and optic nerves—Look, never mind. Really, you saw Theo? Is he well?

Yes, no, I don't know. Did I see him or not?

Ah, well, you may have seen him. But he may not have been there.

Well, can you check?

Check what?

Can't you go to the memory or something to see if he's there or if I just imagined it?

Oh, you might have imagined it. In fact, you probably did. But you'll still have a memory of it.

Yeah, but you can check if it's real, right?

It'll be real. To you. But it mightn't be real to anyone else.

Jules hit his head with his hand. He was sick of his brain. Ask it to do one simple thing and it turned it upside down and into this mind-numbing argument that went nowhere. What use was a brain that made your mind go numb? It was always saying how incredibly superior it was, and how it could do all this stuff, and then it could never answer one simple question.

I can. You've never asked a simple question.

I am right now! Did I see Theo or not?

Define "see."

What was the point of talking to a brain like that? Jules decided then and there that was definitely it. He kept trying to stop talking to his brain, and then he would relent. Now he didn't care what his brain said. He didn't care anymore if everyone was doing it all the time. He didn't care if he needed to ask his brain something to save himself from certain annihilation, he was not going to talk to his brain anymore. He was going to stop. It was childish. This was no way for a nearly-fourteen-year-old to go on. Two years away from being allowed to drive a car. He was no child. He did everything for himself. He cooked, he cleaned, he shopped. He lived with his dad. He got himself over to his mom's. He'd nearly kissed a girl. He was a Time-Jumper. He'd been to the future, he'd been to the past. And right here in the present it was time to grow up.

I agree, said his brain.

Shut up. Go away. I don't want to hear from you again. Go lie down in your office, like you always do when things get weird.

Jules waited for a reply.

There wasn't one.

He waited a bit longer.

Still nothing.

It was a bit eerie not hearing his brain answer back.

Like a sudden silence on a busy road, or in a football crowd. It only happened when there was something wrong.

Missing me?

No!

Jules got up and stomped out of the bathroom and back along the corridor, trying to think of something else. Which isn't possible, because if you try to think of something else, all you can think about is the thing you're trying not to think about. Which is exactly the kind of thing his brain would have pointed out to him, had his brain been there talking to him. So even though his brain wasn't talking to him, Jules was still having the same conversations. He needed a distraction.

Gen was a good distraction. She was walking toward the cafeteria with the girls.

They all smiled at Jules. Jules smiled and frowned and twitched a little in response.

Gen stopped. "I'll catch up with you," she called to the girls.

"You all right?" she said to Jules.

"Yes. No. I don't know." Jules looked up and down the corridor and then leaned over and whispered in Gen's ear. "I just saw Theo!"

"What? Where?"

"In the classroom. Just for a second in the corner of my eye, there he was!"

"You sure?"

"Yes! And then he just started writing on the blackboard to me. And he spoke."

Gen looked a little more closely at Jules. "What did he say?"

"'Gotta go,'" said Jules.

"Theo Jumped in to tell you he'd gotta go?"

"I think he was trying to tell me more than that."

"Would Theo be using the JumpMan at Blast, perhaps?" asked Gen.

Jules stood back from her. "This is really happening, Gen."

"To you, yeah," she replied. "I'm not sure that it's really happening in, like, the real world!"

Great, thought Jules. *Gen's like my brain. Thinks I'm seeing things. Maybe I am seeing things. And hearing them.*

He grabbed her arm. "Come and have a look. He wrote on the blackboard."

Gen followed Jules into the classroom.

A teacher was cleaning the board. "I don't think you two are supposed to be in here," she said.

Jules and Gen walked back out.

Gen put her hand on his arm and came in close to him.

"Sometimes, Jules, you know, Theo and Franklin and the whole TimeJumping thing? I'm not even sure it actually happened. Did we all just dream it at once? And I mean, really, Quincy is going to get us? Why? We're just some kids. We go to school. When the whole TimeJumping thing isn't happening, it's almost like it never happened."

Jules slumped a little further. Great, now Gen was forgetting it all.

"Maybe you should go home, Jules. You can't be thinking about this every second of the day. I can't. It's too much."

Jules did go home, but over the next few days it was no different. He kept on seeing Theo. Only for a second, and only ever out of the corner of his eye, but there he was. Jules was positive. Little cheeky face, bright crimson or gold or deep aqua hair, coat in some kind of wild arrangement—who else but Theo? He noticed that it only ever happened when he was distracted.

Then one day when he was walking into class, he realized he'd forgotten his folder. He turned, and as he did so, he saw Genevieve looking at him, an odd expression on her face. He stopped and looked at her, and she turned away.

What was that about, he thought. Was she looking at

him like she hated him? Was she just looking at him while she thought about something else? Was she looking at him like she was going to tell him something? He couldn't figure it out. But he couldn't just stand there in the doorway, so he took a few steps forward. And then he stopped again and shook his head. What was he doing here, why he was walking away from class?

It was like one of those Magic Eye 3-D things that had been all the rage for about three minutes when Jules was eight. You looked at them and for one second you saw the 3-D picture, and then, a second later, it was just a collection of curvy squiggles again.

Or like yesterday, when Jules had been drifting off in class. Gazing out the window, he'd stopped listening to Mr. Olsen drone on about how over millions of years the movements of the tide formed coastlines. Looking at the dry grass of the playing fields, Jules had started to see the wide open plains of forty thousand years ago, plains he'd seen when he, Theo, and Gen had been TimeJumping. Once again, murderous Neanderthals were bearing down on him. He could taste the dust and smell their animal sweat as they pounded nearer and nearer. And then he recalled the time he'd wandered the universe, in the future, back to the Big Bang, that miraculous few seconds when he'd felt as though he were as small as an atom but as though each atom around him were as big as a galaxy; as though he were hurtling at the speed of light through all eternity, and as though he were absolutely still and not moving at all. He was light, though all else was dark. He seemed invisible, but all around him was brilliance.

And as he remembered that moment, he noticed a slight movement out of the corner of his eye, and there once more was Theo. Again he seemed to be watching Jules, and again he disappeared as soon as Jules became aware of him.

Jules shook his head and realized the whole class was looking at him.

Mr. Olsen was staring at him as well.

"You want to answer the question, Jules, or just spend the afternoon in a state of advanced catatonia?"

The class laughed on cue, and Jules retreated into defensive mumbles and waited for Mr. Olsen to move on.

The bell rang and everyone left. Jules slowly packed up his things. He didn't want to walk out with the others, couldn't be bothered with their jokes and cheap shots.

As he was about to leave, he noticed that a piece of chalk was moving by itself across the blackboard. It was writing his name.

JULES.

So this is what it felt like to go insane. You think chalk can write by itself. Worse, you think it's writing little messages to you.

JUST WAIT HERE. I NEED TO TALK TO YOU. I WON'T RUN OFF THIS TIME.

The chalk settled back in the tray at the bottom of the blackboard. Then it picked itself up again and wrote some more.

RELAX. IT'S ME. THEO

"Theo?" said Jules to an empty classroom.

"Jules," replied the corner of the room in Theo's voice.

"Theo! What is going on? You've gotta help me—"

"Nothing. I'm Jumping everywhere. It's fantastic."

"Where's Quincy? Why are you here?"

"I just thought I should warn you—"

"Warn us? What's happening? Why warn us?"

"Jules! You're very highly strung. I just thought you should know, we haven't found Quincy, Time-Jumping's been suspended, I'm the only one doing it, so you should be careful. Oh, my helix, it's Franklin again, gotta go. I'll leave you messages when I can. Is Gen ever off that phone? I need to talk to her, too."

"Theo, hold on! What do you mean, TimeJumping's

suspended? Are we in danger? What's going on?"

Jules looked around at the six kids who'd filed in for the next class. They were looking at him like he wasn't the coolest kid in school but someone who was deeply disturbed.

Was this it? he thought. *We're about to go Jumping again?*

Jules breathed in deeply. This waiting, the not knowing, was really getting to him. He felt unhinged. Had he just been talking to Theo, or had he imagined the whole thing?

Jules rubbed his name off the board. Theo had written that up there? Or had he written that up there himself? Jules slumped out of the room. He had to get some rest.

THE FUTURE
MONDAY NIGHT FOURTEEN BILLION AND SEVENTY-THREE

Meanwhile, Theo was having a really good time. Sure, Franklin seemed worried that they couldn't find Quincy anywhere, and he and Duncan were worried about TimeJumping being closed down for good, but Theo loved his new job. He was seeing JumpSites as he'd never seen them before. Whenever he'd gone in the past, he'd always been there with a group of his friends, which had been a big part of it. They'd make jokes, fool around, talk, and not really see what was right in front of them. Now it was just him, and he had to have a good look at what was there. He had to report back.

Take Doctor's Surgery 1780. Theo and his friends had always had a blast at this one. In Fourteen Billion and Seventy-three, you were never sick. Your coat monitored your body systems. It could diagnose whatever was happening and fix it up straight away. You ate everything you were meant to, and you got the right amount of exercise. Getting sick just didn't happen. Theo never had a cold until he went to Mil 3.

So going to Doctor's Surgery, when people got really sick and then had to endure treatments that were worse, that was funny in a very sick kind of way. But now that he was there on his own, it was hard to see what they had made jokes about before.

Patients came in and they looked truly ghastly: sweating, feverish, pale, yellow, choked up, in a lot of pain. The doctor would examine them and then heat up some glasses, some ordinary-looking glasses, and then press them to the patient's naked flesh. It really hurt. But the weird thing was that the doctor thought he was helping the patient and the patient seemed grateful for the treatment.

The glasses were hard going, but the leeches were worse. The doctor would peer at the patient in the candlelight, leaning over him or her with a jar of fresh leeches. Then the Doctor would stick them onto the patient's body. The leeches would start sucking with great vigor, and in a few minutes be as fat as glossy cockroaches.

Theo thought he'd seen enough when in the next consultation the doctor started to advise the patient that if the maggots didn't work on his festering wound, the leg would have to be sawn off. Theo thanked his lucky genomes he lived in Fourteen Billion and Seventy-three. He left as the doctor started unscrewing a jar with MAG-GOTS written on it in spidery, inky handwriting. There was only so much you could deal with.

He Jumped on to the next sites on his list. So far nothing was happening. The past was where it should have been—in the past—and everything that had happened was still happening back when it should have happened. The Great Wall of China was still being built and still keeping no one out. The Trojans were still being destroyed because one of their princes had a new girlfriend, earthquakes were still wiping out civilizations, volcanoes were erupting, dinosaurs were still stomping around—all of the past was where it was meant to be.

So Theo would make his rounds and then JumpBack to MeanTime, which was also hugely entertaining. What was it about inventing TimeJumping that had turned its inventors so batty? Quincy was a megalomaniac, Franklin was a total grump, and Duncan was completely obsessed with his own appearance and with time.

Theo could never tell if Duncan was gazing at a clock because he had caught a reflection of himself in it or if he was checking on a potential timeRipple. He seemed to treat both with equal seriousness.

"Come on, Theo, be cruel," he'd demanded when Theo arrived back from checking that Marie Antoinette was still expecting the starving peasants to eat cake instead of bread. "Should I get longer eyelashes? They're short. Stubby, really. I could get it done. Eyelash implant—straight into the booth. Takes three seconds."

Theo agreed and Duncan nodded happily. Next time Theo turned up, perhaps after watching some giant flesh-eating kangaroos bounce around early Australia, Duncan turned to him and said, "Why can't we Jump before the Big Bang?"

Theo looked startled.

"Does it make any sense to you? Really? When you

think about it. Nothing. Then a Big Bang. After Big Bang, everything. Explain that."

He stared at Theo until Theo was unsure whether he'd been sitting for minutes or hours.

"See that?" Duncan pointed upward at a screen that, unlike every other timepiece in the place, had just a single figure on it. It was the number one and it was just coming into view.

"What time is it on that clock?" Duncan asked.

"Just after one?" answered Theo. "Just before one?"

"That is my AllTime Clock," declared Duncan. "That measures All Time but as a unit of one. We always divide time up into smaller and smaller units. What if we didn't? If the click of time from the Big Bang until the end of time was just one time unit? Call it one eternium. Does that mean this is the first and only eternium? There must have been one before. Or maybe a million. Maybe eterniums go on forever. I want to JumpBack to the end of the last eternium. When the universe collapsed again to a single point, before all matter exploded out!"

Theo nodded like he understood. Jump before the Big Bang? Could you do that? He thought about it while he went on Jumping to sites. Off to check that Ali Baba still had forty thieves, off to a string of fabulous places with fabulous names: Timbuktu, Babylon, Nineveh, Ulaanbaatar, Varanasi, Memphis, Machu Picchu. So it was fun. Theo was Jumping again. He was really enjoying Jumping solo, and if Quincy was doing anything nasty to the past, it wasn't very obvious. So far all that had happened, or rather unhappened, was the can opener.

Theo kept visiting Mil 3. He tried to get a message to Gen, but—unless he could figure out how to talk to her phone, it just wasn't going to work.

He'd written GEN, MAKE SURE YOU STICK WITH JULES, LOVE, THEO in large white letters across the window of a store she was walking into, and she'd paid no attention whatsoever. She'd been calling Bonnie to see if she thought Gen should get a new top in red or in blue.

He gave up, and next time, early in the morning, he went to Jules's place and was just about to write a message in the frost on the window when Franklin called.

"You're in Mil 3!" Franklin screamed accusingly.

Theo scrunched up his face. "Yip, yip. I'm just leaving!"

"You're not meant to be there at all!"

"Yip, already. I'm going."

"Get back to MeanTime. It's started."

"What? What's started?"

"Get back here now! We're going to Mars! With a slight detour!"

Franklin hung up.

Theo scrawled quickly. Then he Jumped.

THE PRESENT

WEDNESDAY AFTERNOON EARLY MIL 3

Jules and reality started to become strangers. It was hard to maintain the kind of grip most had on their lives when you kept seeing someone out of the corner of your eye and when messages addressed to you kept appearing in the dirt alongside the footpath, on whiteboards and blackboards, typed up on computer screens, anywhere really that someone invisible from three thousand years in the future could get to and then write you a little note.

And it didn't help Jules's overall feeling of anxiety and nervousness that the messages tended to say things like: JULES. NO SIGN OF QUINCY YET. STILL BE CAREFUL. THEO.

He printed out one he'd found on his computer when he'd got home, and showed it to Gen.

"Theo typed this? Into your computer?" she said.

Jules nodded.

"Are you sure you didn't type this into your computer?"

Jules shrugged. No, he wasn't sure he didn't type it into his own computer. The way he was feeling he might have typed it in, forgotten about it, and then found it five minutes later and been convinced that Theo had done it. But he was sure he hadn't written on the yellow Post-it notes that were stuck all over his mirror one morning, and he was positive he hadn't written in some dust on the way to school, and he was sure that these messages were from Theo.

He couldn't concentrate on anything much. He was losing large slabs of the day as he tried to figure out what was going on. *I'm here and I'm me. But what if I'm not? Either here or me. Maybe that whole parallel universe thing is true.*

Perhaps after the last JumpBack, instead of returning to the world he'd left, he'd Jumped into a parallel universe that was more or less like his own world but had some little points of difference. A world where Jules was cool. A world where Gen had a cell phone. A world where messages could appear at any time from someone called Theo.

How do I know I'm where I'm meant to be? If I'm in a parallel world, who's being me in my own world? Or are there dozens, thousands, or millions of me in different parallel universes all kind of the same but all a little bit different?

Around about now his brain would have piped up, but he'd chased his brain away. *That was a good idea,* he thought sarcastically. *I could really do with my brain now. Perhaps I'm going mad because I don't talk to my brain anymore. Perhaps I was mad when I did talk to my brain, and now I'm going sane.*

As they walked home from school that afternoon, he tried again to talk to Gen about it. Between the calls on her cell phone.

"You sure you haven't seen anything? No messages, no Theo?"

Gen shrugged and turned to answer him. The phone rang.

Gen had been right. Once she'd got one, each of the other girls got one. The nagging power of a fourteen-year-old is a very compelling force. Between every class they'd take them out and self-importantly check their messages. The fact that the messages were from one another didn't matter, they just loved getting them out to check them.

When they didn't call, they texted one another.

2CU:)AM. GR8!

:(NOT.

NOT? Y?

BCOZ I AM GRNDED.BIG:(.

They texted when they were walking away from one another. They kept doing it when they got home. At night they sent each other a little good-night text. Jules had even seen them texting one another as they walked along together.

Gen read the message on her screen now while Jules fumed beside her. She laughed, thought for a moment, and then tapped a message back.

"Seen Theo again?" she asked lightly.

"I just asked you that!"

"Oh, yeah. Um, no, I haven't seen anything," said Gen, not really looking at him. "Jules, you know what I think is happening—oh, hang on."

Gen reached into her pocket, read the screen on her phone again, tapped in a message, and put it back.

Then she turned to Jules once more.

"Kyeela's so funny."

"Great. What do you think is happening?" asked Jules.

"About what?"

"You started to tell me what you thought was really happening—"

But Gen was already reaching into her pocket to pick out her vibrating cell phone.

Jules couldn't believe it. He'd wanted a phone, but Tony had said no way. When he could pay for one, he could have one. And Angela had said she had great concerns about the levels of microwave radiation, and how too much phone use would contribute to the breakdown of real relationships and would put us out of touch with our inner voices. It was very annoying to have a cell phone constantly thrust in his face like this.

"You know, this is just like TimeJumping, really," he said when she finally put the phone away.

"What is?" asked Gen.

"You with the freaking phone. You're here and then you're gone. You're just off somewhere else!"

"What's your problem?"

"Well, we're talking, right? And then you have to answer the phone."

"I'm, like, one second."

"You're, like, not. It's thirty seconds. And then thirty seconds later you have to do it again. And it doesn't stop!"

"It does so," said Gen, reaching into her pocket to pull out the phone. "You're exaggerating. And besides, I can do both. I can talk to you and text Kyeela back."

"You cannot."

But Gen didn't answer. She was texting Kyeela.

"You can't do both," Jules repeated when she had finished. "You just think you can."

They walked on in silence, which was only interrupted by Gen's phone bursting into song.

"Great! It worked!" she cried, holding the phone up and dancing along the street.

"What was that all about?" asked Jules, exasperated at having his point proven but feeling like he was losing the argument anyway.

"Free ringtones!" said Gen. "Kyeela was downloading them and sending them on to me."

Jules stopped. The entire conversation that had gone on while they walked along was about the phone. Jules shook his head. Gen saw him and stopped walking.

"What is the big deal with you?"

"Well, Gen, you know. We're walking along here. We need to talk about the whole TimeJumping thing. And you just keep on pretending that if you ignore it, it'll be like it never happened. It's still happening, you know. Theo is Jumping in. We've got to be ready."

"Jules, I can't do it. I don't want them to Jump in again. I don't want to see them. I don't want to hear about them."

Her phone rang.

"Yes!" she said excitedly into the phone. "It sounds so cool, doesn't it? I mean, these new ringtones really rock."

Jules couldn't believe it. Now it was just so exciting that they had to talk about it. A conversation on the phone about the phone. They were talking about the sound the phone made when it rang. And he thought *he* was going mad?

They stopped outside her house.

And for the first time in months there seemed to be nothing to say. Gen broke the slience.

"Look, Jules. We're friends, right?"

"Yeah. Of course."

"And we'll always be good friends, right?"

"Yeah. What are you talking about?"

"I just think maybe we should just be good friends, you know?"

"Well, we are good friends. Aren't we?"

"Of course. But the whole, you know, boyfriend thing. Maybe that's just not working."

Jules was silent for a moment.

"Were we—are we boyfriend-girlfriend?"

"Sure. Didn't you think we were?"

"I didn't know."

"Jules?"

"Yes?"

"Well? What do you think?"

"Are you . . . are you dropping me? Am I dropped?"

"No! God, Jules. We're good friends. I wouldn't drop you. I just think we should be friends and not worry so much about the boyfriend-girlfriend thing."

"So, I'm dropped. We're not going out anymore?"

"We can still go out. We're not 'going out,' but we're still good friends. I really like you, Jules, and this shouldn't change anything, okay?'

"Has this got anything to do with TimeJumping?"

"It's got everything to do with TimeJumping, Jules."

Gen gave him a sad smile and then turned and went into her house.

Jules walked home and tried to reconstruct the conversation, but after a while it seemed more complicated than the kind of conversations you'd have with Theo or Franklin about time. They were friends and could go out but were not "going out." She really liked him and they were best friends, but not boyfriend and girlfriend. Not that he was dropped. Because they were too good as friends.

Jules slept particularly badly that night. And when he woke up, Theo had written in the frost on his window: GONE 2 MARS CU SOON.

THE PAST

NEAR MIDDAY, HALF-MOON 13,000 BC OLD TIME

After the humiliation of the last meeting, Bug Lover, Two Brow, and Star Speck had spent a lot of time trying to improve the wheel. Two Brow and Star Speck were like Bug Lover; they'd thought all you'd have to do would be to show everyone the wheel and they'd all want it. So they started trying new things out.

Star Speck was there with Fleck, a gangly-looking wolf cub with a head too big for her body and feet too big for her legs. She flopped about and rarely took her eyes off Star Speck. Fleck had been only a few months old when Star Speck brought her right into the village and started caring for her. He'd kept her warm and fed her on goat's milk and meat scraps. The cub had responded by never leaving his side. The others had responded by treating Star Speck as if a thick branch had fallen on his head.

"You know that's a wolf?" they'd say.

"Ya!" Star Speck would say, grinning.

"You know it's going to get bigger?"

"Ya!"

"Then it will eat you."

"Na!"

Star Speck would look at them, a slightly dim grin on his face but total confidence in his eyes, and even though his critics were sure they were speaking the truth, it was they who backed off, feeling doubtful. Star Speck gave every impression that he knew what he was doing.

"She thinks I'm her mother," he explained.

"You?" said Bug Lover. "You don't have pointy ears. You're lacking a wet black nose. You're not a wolf."

"Neither is she," said Star Speck.

"What—"

"She thinks she's human. She doesn't know she's a wolf. All she's seen is me. And us. She doesn't even know other wolves exist. By the time she's fully grown, she'll do whatever I want her to."

Bug Lover had to concede that there were times when he thought Fleck was listening, and it was strange the way Star Speck could get her to come or stay when he needed her to.

"You know, I've been sleeping so well since I got her," said Star Speck. "I don't worry about anything attacking me, or anyone trying to kill me in the night anymore. She sleeps at the door of my shelter and growls if anyone comes near."

Two Brow understood what Star Speck was doing.

She had some pretty strange ideas as well about the animals in the valleys and forests around them. But hers were inherited. She came from a family famous along the Long River for one peculiar ambition. Two Brow's grandfather and father had both tried to sit on the back of the long-faced beasts, the horses that wandered in large packs into the next valley when the grass was long and green.

Everyone knew the story. It was very popular and got told often. How Two Brow's father's father, Flat Head, had gone out with his brother Stone and a few of their friends and instead of hunting the horses had crept up on them. The men had walked among them, and the long-faces had moved quietly away, blowing hot steamy air out of their flaring nostrils, stamping the ground, and harrumphing a bit, but otherwise unconcerned with the humans' presence.

Until Flat Head had grabbed one by the mane of hair along its neck and swung himself up on its back. The long-faced beast was so astonished that for a moment it didn't do anything, but a second later its entire body arched, it leaped straight up into the air, and Flat Head flew off its back to land, winded, on the ground quite a distance away. The horse and the rest of the mob had taken fright, and they'd all galloped off to the other end of the clearing. There they stopped, stomped the ground, harrumphed, and whinnied, looking back at the men.

Flat Head looked up at the sky completely dazed. The other men gathered around him. They stared at him for a moment and then one started to laugh. Soon they were all whooping away. Some slapped their legs; a couple had to sit down. One pointed at the horse and then at Flat Head, and then he traced Flat Head's path through the air, and that set them all off again. Flat Head lay on his back, still a little winded, listening to them laugh at him but mainly lost in thought about his daring moment.

His friends turned around and walked back to the village. By the time they got there, the story had grown; Flat Head had flown twice as high and landed three times farther away, and the horses had come to snigger at him as well.

A little later Flat Head's wife, Smooth Hair, had come to look for him. Flat Head was still in the clearing, but sitting up and watching the horses. Smooth Hair sat down next to him.

"How long were you on for?" she asked.

"There was a moment," he said. "A moment. A heartbeat or two. But I was on, I was on its back."

"Good for you, Flat Head," said Smooth Hair, putting her arm around him and helping him up. "You want to try riding something else, you go right ahead."

Flat Head didn't, but Clear Eye made a painting of the event in the painting cave and Flat Head couldn't believe it when he first saw it.

"Wow!" he said. "Great pictures! Terrific quality!"

"Hope you don't mind me making it into a picture," said Clear Eye.

"It's just got it all. Action, romance—although I did beef up the ending a bit. That's why it looks like you broke your neck."

Mind? Flat Head couldn't believe that his story had been made into an actual picture.

It meant, of course, that everyone knew his story, like they knew the story of the Winter Without Fire or Why the Sun God Burns Your Eyes Out When You Look at Him. So of course what choice did his own son have but to try to ride the horse as well?

Long Lobes had made it across the field, hanging on until the horse bucked and threw him into the prickly bushes on the other side. His story—Horse Ride Two—had been the most popular painting Clear Eye had ever made.

"People love horse pictures," Clear Eye raved. "Can't get enough of 'em."

With this kind of family history, what choice did Two Brow have? Only she was a girl, and no one expected her to attempt it, and unlike her ancestors Two Brow was in no hurry. She loved the horses and spent all the time she could sitting in the grass watching them, letting them get used to her, and thinking about how one day she'd gallop from one end of the valley to the other and amaze everyone.

When Two Brow wasn't watching the horses, she would often be a horse, imitating the different ways they ran and walked. She'd toss her head like they did and try to make their sounds.

"I think to ride one you've almost got to be one," she said. Two Brow thought that day wouldn't be far off now. There was one long-faced she'd noticed that seemed gentler and quieter than the rest. He seemed to know her now, and whenever she was with them, she'd take a special piece of fruit for him.

"My family's always rushed into this thing," she said. "That's been the mistake. I'm going to take my time, and when I think the horse is good and ready, I'm going to give it a try. You wait. It's going to work this time."

She often went to look at the old cave pictures of her father and grandfather. Certainly Clear Eye's son, Ochre Boy, encouraged her to carry on the family tradition.

"I think it's time to bring back the horse picture," he'd say. "But update it, make it work for these more modern times. The old ones are classic, but they've had their day. Don't s'pose you'd like to ride a mammoth, would you? I hear mammoth pictures are going to be big this summer."

Two Brow ignored him. "When you see what I'm going to do on this horse, you'll get your picture."

And while they played with the wolf and thought about the horse, Two Brow and Star Speck spent a lot of time rolling the wheel around, helping Bug Lover figure out exactly what you could do with it.

Nothing happened for some time, until one day Bug Lover and Two Brow were having a wheel race. Star Speck was the judge. They each pushed their wheel off, and Star Speck watched to see whose wheel would reach the line first.

"Both at the same time. They crossed together!" called out Star Speck. Fleck barked and chased the wheels until they fell over.

A strange look came over Star Speck's face. He stared at Bug Lover.

"They crossed together," he repeated slowly. "Together."

"What's wrong with you?"

Star Speck got the wheels and came back and stood them up, side by side, a yard or so apart in front of Bug Lover.

"Together!"

Bug Lover was taking a while to catch on.

"Together!" repeated Star Speck. "We need to run the wheels together, and then it's like a rolling log, only better."

Bug Lover's eyes widened. He saw it. And in fact, he saw in his mind's eye something more.

A few weeks later Bug Lover stood in front of the Meeting Hill again.

"Hello! Hello again! Yes, it's me. Bug Lover!" said Bug Lover from the bottom of the hill.

After the mess of the last time, he was astonished that anyone had turned up. But this time the tribes seemed almost eager to see what Bug Lover had. Watching Bug Lover demonstrate things was one of their favorite entertainments. Outside of going to the pictures. But that only took a few minutes whenever Ochre Boy had come up with a new version of the hunt, or blown a few more handprints in his cave. Bug

Lover and his crackpot theories and newfangled ideas were a huge snort, and so no wonder he was popular.

"You mean Wheel Lover, don't you?" someone called out, and a few in the crowd grunted and snorted and banged the side of their heads in appreciation.

"All right. Wheel Lover. I suppose I am." Bug Lover smiled, happy to agree with them, glad so many had come along.

"Well. When we were all last here, Moon Smacked asked me what this was for, and I must admit I hadn't really thought about how to use it. I was just so amazed at its rolling, I thought you'd all like to see that. So over the last few moons, Two Brow, Star Speck, and I have been working hard and well. We've come up with this. Roll it in, guys."

It wasn't one wheel that rolled in. It was two. And the two wheels were connected. But that wasn't all.

The two wheels were attached to a flat tray with two long sticks coming off it. Two Brow was pulling the contraption along by the two sticks.

Star Speck pushed in another version with four wheels and a flat wooden tray on the top. He pushed it, and it rolled over to the other side of the clearing. The crowd watched it go in astonished silence.

"Um, so that's it," said Bug Lover. "You can carry

things on there, push them around. We think it'll be easier and faster than the old log rolling system."

There was some murmuring and grunting, but no one was screaming and no one was throwing spears yet. Then a skinny member of the Tribe on the High Hill stood up and came forward. He went over to the cart and spat on it.

"I am a log roller. My father was a log roller. His father was a log roller. We have always log rolled. Log rolling is how you move things. You want to move something, you put one log in front of another and then bring the ones at the back around to the front. This thing will be the end of log rolling. I say Bug Lover is evil and should be eaten next full moon."

Skinny Bones sat down. There was a lot of grunting and nodding from his friends. Some of them licked their lips. Another one stood up.

"Skinny Bones is right," he declared. "We are the stick draggers. They have put wheels on a stick dragger. The god of sticks will be angry and we'll all starve. I too want to eat Bug Lover. And those other two."

Things had got nasty pretty fast. Bug Lover had expected some opposition, but he hadn't expected to be a candidate for dinner quite so soon. Fleck growled softly at Star Speck's feet. Two Brow tried to fade into the darkness but just ended up looking strange and could feel everyone watching her.

Moon Smacked leapt up at this point.

"Friends! I asked Bug Lover what you would do with the wheel. He's come up with a trick. He says his trick will make things faster and easier. Faster? Can you make the river run faster? The sun move faster? Why make things faster? What will you do when you get there?"

Lots of pleased grunting at that one. Good point.

"Yes!" said another, picking up the theme. "I think only log rollers or stick draggers should be allowed to use the new wheel, if we even decide to use the wheel at all. Unless Bug Lover is proposing that his tribe should start carrying things around instead of the log rollers or the stick draggers?'

An angry buzz swelled up about that.

Bug Lover tried to get their attention and tell them again that the wheel was for everyone, but he couldn't be heard. The noise grew until a short man, covered in thick black hair and about as wide as he was high, stood up. They all went quiet.

"I don't wanna see no one get hurt."

The short man paused and everyone hoped he wouldn't look at them.

"But it hurts me when I hear someone sayin' there's

sumpin' wrong with log rolling. It hurts me when I see someone take some sticks and put some little wheels on them."

You could have heard a bone needle drop.

"I don't like being hurt. I guess you guys don't either. Which is why I'm guessin' you don't wanna get into the carryin' business. Which I run from here to the Mountains Where the Pink Mushrooms Grow. Right?"

Bug Lover gave a tiny nod of his head. This was serious.

"The last person who thought they could take some of my carryin' business made a very nice bone marrow stew. You guys don't want to be bone marrow stew. Right?"

They all gave tiny shakes of the head. This was Blackhair talking. He was the nastiest, toughest, most sadistic, meanest guy in the whole Long River. And for a tribe of recently reformed cannibals, that was really saying something.

Everyone stared at Bug Lover and his friends. Fleck seemed to know that now wasn't the time to growl, so she stayed lying flat on the ground.

Bug Lover was suprised how young and shaky his voice sounded all of a sudden. "I don't want to carry things. I'm not trying to take over anything. The wheel is for everyone. You can do what you like with it."

Someone else stood up at the back. "Are your wheels going to be compatible with my logs, or will I have to upgrade my logs?"

Good question. Excellent question. Bug Lover wished he'd thought of an answer before now. Better be confident.

"Yes!" he shouted. "Of course. We'll do the conversion for you!"

Another stood up. "Does the wheel have to be round? It seems to me that if it wasn't round, then we wouldn't be having all of these arguments. So why not make the wheel more square-shaped, or something?"

Bug Lover felt a pain in his temples, and he wanted nothing more than to go back to his scrape in the ground, take two pieces of tannin bark with a handful of water, and wait until the pain went away. If pain persisted he could always go and see the witch doctor tomorrow.

Why was it that so often people seemed to get only half the idea? And whenever they did, it was always the wrong half?

It was all becoming too much for Bug Lover. Couldn't they see how miraculous the wheel was? The criticism kept on coming. Maybe there should be only six wheels and that's all. Maybe one tribe could have one of the little carts for a few moons to see if it was safe. Maybe the wheels should only be made a certain size, not so big as to threaten log rolling but big enough to move a little bit of grain around or for children to play on.

Then there was a great argument about how old you should be before you could use the wheel. Should it be part of initiation? Should women be allowed to use the wheel? The men all agreed that women would be hopeless wheel users, and wanted them banned from it. Unless of course they decided that women could have the wheel, and then it wouldn't matter. It would just be a woman's thing like a grinding stone, and who would care what happened to it?

Bug Lover looked out at the crowd. He held his hands up.

"Quiet! Quiet, please. There's something I want to say."

Apart from a few who'd forgotten about the wheel and were now discussing tomorrow's game of Club the Goat, everyone looked at Bug Lover.

"All right. I don't have all the answers. But I'm not trying to take over anyone else's role. Or roll," he added, but went straight on as he knew even Two Brow wouldn't get that one. "I'm not interested. I don't care. The wheel is yours. You can have it. It's free. Do what you like with it. Don't do anything with it. The point is, it's here now, and anyone can use it. Look at these ones."

Star Speck stepped forward with a handful of small wheels on the end of a stick. They were attached to some rope.

"See? We made these as models, but then when we hung them on a rope we noticed that you just had to hit one every now and again and it spun for quite a long time."

Star Speck demonstrated. A few of the other tribesmen grunted loudly and nodded a bit. It was a good trick.

"What do you do with that, then?"

It was Moon Smacked once more. And once more he'd punctured the mood with his perfectly reasonable but, to Bug Lover's mind, incredibly annoying question.

"I don't know!" he snapped, angry this time. "Whatever you want to do with it! Look at it. We made it. We can make it do this. Maybe tomorrow we'll think of other ways to use it. But don't you see? Don't you see the real point of all this? The world has now changed forever. The world is now different from the way it was yesterday. The world now has the wheel and nothing will ever be the same again."

chapter four
TIME POOR

THE PRESENT

THURSDAY NIGHT EARLY MIL 3

It was odd walking into the school with his mom and dad. Jules hadn't seen them together like this, like other moms and dads, for a couple of years now. But here they were just in front of him, walking along, and they were talking. They smiled at each other, and for a moment he could imagine that they were a family, still together and like all of the other still-together families walking into the school for this term's Parent-Teacher-Student Performance Evaluation, Negotiation, and Approbation Night.

At the very least his separated parents looked happier than most of the other separated parents. Glance at half of them and you got the feeling that there was no greater torment in the world than having to spend an hour or so together.

Jules and Tony had gone to pick up Angela. She was back in town now with her new baby and a new—a new what?

"What does Angela call Celeste when she's speaking to you?" Tony had asked in the car on the way over. "Significant other? Co-renter? Housemate? Person to call in case of accident? Kith? Maybe she's kith. You know, like kith and kin? Kin is family, but I've never been clear who kith were."

Jules didn't like to think about Celeste too much. It had been hard enough when his mother had had a new boyfriend, but now—a new . . . ?

Jules waited for a moment. He was waiting for his brain to speak up. Usually it would have chimed in by now and supplied him with the word. But all was silent up there. It made Jules feel much better. Or it made him feel much worse. He couldn't tell.

This morning's message from Theo had completely unsettled him. CU SOON? Soon. Now? Where was he? Jules had been trying all week to get back to Blast to see if he could find the JumpMan, but that was going to have to wait until the weekend. There was just no resolving any of this. And now a parent-teacher night. Perfect. Could it get any worse?

Gen walked in, with Steven and Katherine. That was

the only other thing on his mind. Gen. What was going on with her? He knew she was as worried as he was, but she seemed so determined not to show it.

He and his parents went over to their first teacher. Mr. Olsen. Perfect. The geography class he'd been asleep in.

Mr. Olsen gave them a quick professional smile through his bushy beard and indicated two chairs for Tony and Angela.

"Nice to have you here, Mrs. Santorini—," he began.

"Please, I don't mean to be difficult, but I no longer recognize the patrinominal matrimonial title," she replied. "It makes me feel like a possession. I am an entity unto myself and answerable only to the cosmos. We are also divorced. I'm known now only as Angela."

"All right, then, Angela. Well, Jules—" And there he stopped and looked at Jules for a moment and down at what he'd written. He began to read from his notes.

"Jules is forming a learning relationship with the core material of the required curriculum. He is addressing the central issues of the course and displaying a cognitive connection to the problems and information as presented. He, ahh . . ." Mr. Olsen petered out.

He tucked his tongue behind his teeth and then

looked from Tony to Angela and back for a moment or two.

"Jules hasn't really been with us for a while now. Everything all right at home?"

Jules's jaw dropped. What a terrific start to the evening.

"Not *with you*? What do you mean?" asked Tony. "Not at school?"

"Oh yes, he's been present. He's been sitting in his chair. I just don't think he's heard a word I've said. Am I being unfair, Jules?"

"What?" said Jules, who'd been deep in thought about how he was going to have to explain all this when he got home and how boring that was going to be.

"See what I mean?" said Mr. Olsen.

Angela joined in. "I think you may need to think about what you're teaching," she said. "Boys need to find their masculinity in a society increasingly hostile to their needs. Do you have any kind of initiation rites here?"

"Well, there is camp in term three, but I wouldn't say we had initiation rites—"

"And so how does a young boy know what the elders of his tribe want for him? And then there's diet. How do they concentrate when they eat slaughtered beasts made fat from genetically modified grain filled with drugs that suppress their natural libido?"

Even Tony and Jules, who were used to Angela's preoccupations, were finding this one a bit hard to follow.

Mr. Olsen stood up. "Look, I've written him a fine report, as I can see Jules has all the potential to do well at this subject. I'm just letting you know. I see him every day, and the lights are on but no one is home at the moment. Okay? Nice to see you. See you at the end of the year."

It didn't get any better.

Jules slumped down in front of his English teacher, who informed his parents that he'd handed in excellent work at the start of the year and nothing in the last month. How were things at home, she asked.

Angela didn't hesitate, picking straight up from where she'd left off with Mr. Olsen. "How can a system like this, which treats them all as little robots, ever be expected to find the true person, the soul, the psyche, the expression of a humanity which is the expression of stardust come to Earth?"

The English teacher nodded and suggested that perhaps Jules should see a doctor to make sure he didn't have glandular fever, depression, diabetes, chronic fatigue syndrome, allergies, or a range of conditions that might explain his suddenly poor performance.

Jules turned around. There was Gen. And Katherine and Steven and Cynthia.

"Well, hello!" said all the adults way too brightly, to cover their awkwardness. Angela hadn't seen the Corrigans since her return, and this was not really the place to meet up for the first time.

"Going well?" they asked, indicating the teachers and Jules.

"Terrific," said Tony and Angela. "Very pleased." And they gave Jules's shoulders a squeeze. "You? How's Gen doing?"

"Well, we're really a bit blown away. It seems like she's been working a bit harder than I would have thought," said Steven. "I thought she was just on the phone all the time, but it seems like she's done some actual work, here and there."

"Well, she's certainly grown, and is that Cynthia?" said Angela. "She's so big now! What is she, seven?"

"Seven and a half now," replied Steven.

It's strange, isn't it, thought Jules, *the way adults always seem astonished that time has passed.* You would think seeing as how they were kind of old, they might have noticed by now that years go by and, as they do, kids grow up. They get taller, they go to high school. They stop playing with trains and become capable of playing the guitar. Jules wondered why adults always seemed astonished that you weren't exactly as you were three or four years ago. In fact, if you were exactly as you'd been three or four years ago, then that would be a good reason for being astonished. *But then again,* he thought, *years go by and adults don't seem to change much. They just stay old. Perhaps they think kids should just stay young.*

"You're happy with the school?" asked Angela.

"It's a very good school," said Katherine. "We're very happy with it."

Why don't you go to it, then? thought Jules.

"Principal is very good. Some terrific teachers." *Really?* thought Jules. *Have you seen Ms. Aquilera? She could make the Super Bowl sound dull.* Jules was enjoying his pondering. He was doing what his brain usually did.

The school conversation had run out. The adults were starting to look desperate. They slapped their hands together and looked about for an excuse to move.

"I think the math line isn't too bad now, so we might head over for more good news!" Tony said, and laughed.

"All right, then," said Steven.

Jules slid into the seat like a sad slug and stared at the floor. His parents weren't much more enthusiastic.

They weren't really looking forward to hearing once again how Jules had been walking around in a coma for the last month or so.

"Yip. These two yours, then? Oak-I, let's Jump!"

Jules's head shot up. Now he knew he was finally, completely, and utterly insane. Where his math teacher should have been was Franklin. Sitting next to him was Theo.

You're seeing them! They're really there! It's them.

Jules ignored the sudden resurgence of his brain.

"Excuse me, I didn't quite catch that," said Tony.

"Hey, Dodoboy," said Theo, grinning from ear to ear. "Did you get my messages?"

"Dodoboy?" said Angela. "Could I ask why there is another student sitting here. And even though I love his hair, I don't think it's appropriate, do you?"

"Hmm?" grunted Franklin. "Where's Gen?"

"Over there," said Jules, suddenly feeling quite light and happy. They were here! They were actually here. "Are we going to Jump soon?" he asked as Theo got up and went over and tapped Gen on the shoulder. Jules watched her turn around and nearly faint.

"Just need Gen and her parents," said Franklin, looking around. "Just trying to keep it quiet. Don't want everyone to notice."

Tony leant forward.

"Are you Jules's math teacher? I don't think I caught your name."

"Franklin. Franklin Nixon One. I'm not. His math teacher. Explain in a minute."

Gen came over with Theo, her parents, and Cynthia behind her.

"Franklin!" she exclaimed. "Not now. I don't want to go now."

"No choice." Franklin shrugged. "You ready?"

"It's him, it's him. It's the boy with the hair!" Gen's mom, Katherine, was in ecstasy. A bit like Jules, she was suddenly feeling good. There was the boy who always popped up whenever she started to lose it and think that the kids were appearing and disappearing. Only now, she was looking straight at the boy with the wild hair and he wasn't going anywhere. So either she was losing her mind again, which she really quite enjoyed, or she wasn't losing her mind and there really was a boy with wild hair right in front of her.

"Yip, that everyone?" Theo looked at Jules and Gen.

"Franklin—," yelled Gen.

"Can you keep it down? I'm hoping we can Jump to Mars without anyone else noticing."

"Keep it down? What's going on? Why are you here—," Gen began to protest.

"No time!" said Franklin.

They all Jumped.

THE PAST
MIDWINTER EVENING, FULL MOON 13,000 BC OLD TIME

The moon had risen behind the hill several hours earlier. It was now full and quite high in the clear night sky. Once again the tribes had gathered. Once again a speaker stood illuminated at the bottom of the Meeting Hill. There was great eagerness to hear what he had to say. But this time it wasn't Bug Lover who'd gathered them together. This time it was Moon Smacked who'd started the whisper to be here this moon, for he had much he wanted to say about this new idea, the wheel. And now it was he holding up his hands for silence.

"Elders, witch doctors, tribesmen of the Long River, unaffiliated forest-fringe dwellers, the few remaining Neanderthals, and those without words, good evening." Moon Smacked was wearing his best skin. His partner had picked most of the lice from his beard, and the gristle from his teeth. He was standing up to his full yard-and-a-half height and was an imposing sight.

"Over the last few moons Bug Lover has been here, showing us his wheel. He has demonstrated it, has made a few slight suggestions for how it might be used. He has even offered it to us all, and said that it was ours. We could use it. It didn't belong to him. Or to his tribe. It belonged to us all."

Moon Smacked's gaze swept over the assembly. He was speaking well. He'd gone up away from the village and rehearsed his speech among the birds, and they had seemed to like it too.

"I say, I have never seen such a blatant act of war and treachery in all my life. Had Bug Lover come and urinated on my goat"—a particularly insulting gesture—"I could not be more offended or suspicious."

Moon Smacked had their attention now—even the Flatheads up at the back knew the word "war"—and in particular he had Bug Lover's.

Bug Lover had of course heard the whisper, calling the meeting, and he'd been wondering just what Moon Smacked was planning. It had never occurred to him that Moon Smacked would take this line. He glanced at Two Brow and Star Speck, who'd gone white at Moon Smacked's words.

"Sorry, guys," muttered Bug Lover. "It looks like we are going to be eaten after all."

"This is an attack! An attack on our way of life!" Moon Smacked revved up the intensity. "Bug Lover says, 'Take my wheel.' Why? Because it will weaken us. The noble traditions of log rolling will be lost. The little wheels will start to spin and mash and pound, and soon our skills of making rope and grinding wheat with rocks will be gone. Our women will sit idle. Our children will have nothing to do. They will grow fat and lazy and we will be a soft target. And it's not the tribes from over the hills I'm worried about."

Moon Smacked paused for dramatic effect.

"I'm worried about Bug Lover and his lot. We'll be weak, and it will be the perfect opportunity for the Tribe That Cannot Hunt to come and take everything from us. All because of his wheel. His stupid, unnecessary, and treacherous wheel!"

There was a great roar from the crowd. Some of them stood up and banged their hands together. Bug Lover noticed that and thought, *That's it! When people approve of something, they should bang their hands together.* He tried it a few times and then worked out it was easier and less painful if you did it with your hands open and flat rather than with clenched fists. Then he saw that Two Brow and Star Speck were now faint with fear, and he realized that he'd better think of something soon, or the wheel would be finished and they would be dead.

"Look at the moon," ranted Moon Smacked. "The wheel is the shape of the moon! What if we offend the moon god by making such a thing here on Earth? By bringing the moon to the ground? The moon god might send disease and dry our water holes and send snakes into our caves!"

Bug Lover rolled his eyes. Why do they always do this? Whenever someone doesn't like something, they always find a god somewhere who's going to be deeply offended. So sensitive, those gods. They're immortal, aren't they? Surely they've got something better to do than be miffed all the time.

Moon Smacked stood as the hand-banging grew in volume.

"I say destroy the wheel. Burn it. Burn the wheel and never, never let it be made again!"

They all stood, and roared and grunted and howled at the moon.

Bug Lover ran down front.

The crowd all spat.

Which mainly meant they spat on the head of the person in front of them. Which of course annoyed the person in front of them, but they didn't blame the spitter—they blamed Bug Lover.

Bug Lover felt their hate, but he realized he didn't have much choice.

"Friends!" he shouted. "Friends, please. I won't keep you from a nice hot hollowed rock of warm goat curd. But let me just suggest this. Maybe Moon Smacked is right. Maybe me and my tribe, who fix your fences and mind your crops and try to make things better for everyone, maybe we've come up with a deadly weapon called the wheel, and when you are weak like a bleating kid, we will come and fight you. Frankly, I hope you're not weak, I hope you're already dead. I mean, look at me—that's the only way I could ever beat any of you in a fight!"

A lot of the crowd snorted and choked at that one. Bug Lover was pleased. He was starting to read the crowd better and figure out what they liked.

"So, I've got an idea."

He waited until they were all quiet.

"Next moon we'll gather back here. Everyone comes back here. And we'll ask everyone if they want to keep the wheel, and those who can count will count how many do. Then we'll ask who wants to destroy the wheel. And the counters can count them. If the number of people who want it destroyed is larger than the number of people who want to keep it, then let's burn it up.

But if more people want to keep it, then we keep it. Simple, eh? Me and Moon Smacked, we've got a whole moon to come and talk to you about it. You've got a moon to think about it. And then we decide. Whatever most people want, that's what all of us will do. Moon Smacked, what do you think? Think you can win that?"

Moon Smacked leapt up immediately. "Sure, Bugsie. I mean, look at them. They hate you and your wheel. Lucky for you it's only the wheel we're gonna burn!"

Bug Lover and Moon Smacked slapped the back of their hands against each other to indicate they had a deal. Bug Lover tried not to wince, but it always hurt whenever they did that. He'd have to think about some new way of confirming an agreement. Perhaps they could slap the front of each other's hands up above their heads. Anyway, that was something for later. Right now he had one moon to convince as many people as possible that the wheel was a good idea.

THE FUTURE
TUESDAY MIDMORNING FOURTEEN BILLION AND SEVENTY-THREE

It was a beautiful day under a soft pink sky, with just the right amount of faint yellow cloud drifting through to provide some contrast. Purplish grasses waved in a gentle breeze. A light scent from the ProtPlant groves gave the warm air a slightly meaty tang, like a distant barbecue.

People zipped by in cars that appeared to be something between a suit and a surfboard. It was a normal day on Mars, and everyone was enjoying it. Except for the small group of people standing on an outer terrace about halfway up the 840-story United Planets grow tower. They were in an extreme state of shock.

"Welcome to Mars," said Franklin with a little wave of his hand. Something resembling a grin had formed in the creases of his face.

"Hello?" he called, and waved a little more vigorously. "I'm here in front of you." But no one was really paying him any attention. Jules, Gen, Cynthia, their parents, and even Theo were all transfixed by whatever their eyes landed on. Nothing around them looked like anything they'd ever seen before. Everything had to be sorted into categories, and there were too many things refusing to be sorted at all. The color of the sky and the clouds, the height of the buildings, the impossibly high mountain off in the distance, the vehicles buzzing by, the look and costumes of the people passing through, the ground far below them, the sounds, the smells, the feel of the air; there was absolutely nothing that resembled home, school, or any other part of early Mil 3 planet Earth.

"Yip, all a bit strange, I know," continued Franklin, doing a reasonable impression of a genial host and tour guide. "It takes a bit of getting used to. The main thing is that funny sensation of drag around the feet, don't you think? That's artificial gravity, and it just feels completely different. It still takes me a day or two to get accustomed to it, and I'm always happiest when I get back to Earth. Anyone listening yet?"

Jules was staring at Franklin but, like the rest of them, was not really taking in anything much. And he and Gen were at least used to TimeJumping. For their parents, this was their first Jump. And it wasn't even to somewhere on Earth.

They continued to gaze around them, mouths open, eyes wide, completely lost in contemplation of their surroundings. It was hardly surprising that they were surprised: From the four hundred and fifteenth floor of the United Planets grow tower, they were looking at the first terraformed planet in the solar system.

Everything on Mars was biological. The building they were standing in was a genetically modified tree. The trunk was the main tower, and it was about as big as four city blocks back on Earth in their time. The branches grew out flat and wide and formed stories and platforms, and links to other grow towers nearby. They were standing in a city of enormous buildings that resembled a forest planted by giants. It was a marvelous development of the terraformers, who realized that the entire surface of Mars would have to be covered by trees and plants in order to create a thick and resilient enough atmosphere to sustain life. And so, they developed these giant trees, manipulating their growth patterns to make them habitable, and creating a vast forest of oxygen-producing factories across the planet.

The deep roots of the tree found underground water supplies, drawing them to the surface for their own consumption and to be tapped by a thirsty populace. They could be shaped to any position desired; these photosynthesizing giants were really just like massive bonsai, only they grew about ten thousand times faster and about a million times bigger than a silky oak in a pot in Old Time Japan.

"Well, look. Love to fill you in on everything, but as usual we just don't have the time!" said Franklin. "So, come on. I'm going to take you to our leader!"

Franklin moved toward a doorway, but then had to come back and round everyone up. Tony was still staring at the grow tower buildings with a puzzled look on his face, and Steven was watching the Body-Cars zip by.

Franklin came over and stood next to Steven. "They're cars. Just like yours. Our car designers realized a long time ago that you don't drive a car, you wear a car. You get the car that you think you look good in. So here on Mars we make them more like suits. You zip yourself in, and you can have any color or shape you like. Yip, yip, they're very cool and everyone loves them. Can we get going now?"

Franklin tugged at Steven and tried to move him on. Steven kept staring outward, but his feet moved toward the door.

Gen was watching people. She wanted to scream at Franklin and demand that he Jump them back home again, but as usual with TimeJumping, along with the fear came the fascination. She was on Mars, three thousand years in the future, and it was hard to focus on anything else.

People's clothes—right down to their shoes and socks and the bangles on their wrists—were all changing right in front of her. She was used to Theo's coat and the way you could dial up any costume you wanted, but this was different. Someone would walk onto the terrace wearing a yellow top with two pockets.

Someone else would see this, and *their* top would change to be a yellow top with two pockets. This would have a ripple effect through all of the people walking onto the terrace, until it would hit someone who only had one pocket. The one pocket fashion would ripple back through everyone until someone decided to go a kind of light orange with no pockets. People were creating and following fashion at the speed of light.

Eight midsize nanobots appeared.

"Franklin Nixon One. You are late for the United Planets Sub-Bunch Commission of Inquiry into TimeJumping. And you've brought TimeIntruders with you. Come with us. You're in a lot of trouble."

The nanobots surrounded them and marched them down a long corridor. After a few moments Jules could hear a strange hum and buzz. This noise grew louder, and then suddenly the walls of the corridor dissolved away, the hallway opened out and up, and they were marched smack into the middle of the United Planets Sub-Bunch Commission of Inquiry into TimeJumping.

Inside this space, which ballooned out all around and above them, were hundreds of people. They were gathered in groups, they were talking intently in pairs, they were floating on strange chair-desk combinations above their heads.

The hum and buzz that Jules had heard as they approached was now an intense roar, as though a thousand radios were all playing at full volume but slightly off the station. The noise seemed to hack into their heads, and they were all standing in the middle of this now with their hands over their ears.

But their ears were not the only things being assaulted. Their eyes were also being subjected to a sight that made no sense at all. Running between all the groups of people and around the floating chairs and through the whole of this vast chamber were streams of intense color. At one point the streams poured into a broad river that flowed across the floor and washed up around the walls, before it broke up into hundreds of tiny creeks and tributaries. These smaller creeks of eye-splitting pink and yellow, or deep black and purple, rose into the air and made rapid colored swirls.

The room was flowing with information. Raw, pure information.

The colored streams rushed by so fast they glowed and gleamed. It was like watching a freeway at night, only there were no cars, just the lights. Past their bewildered eyes flowed audio, video, photographs, drawings, words, numbers, recordings, documents, letters, reports, descriptions, and accounts, all broken down, converted into a stream of digits, and pumped through this room like neon blood pulsing through invisible veins.

Jules felt a kind of breathless excitement, although he couldn't have said why. He could see Gen and Theo were reacting in the same way, exhilarated and suddenly a bit hyper, as if they were a couple of a five-year-olds with a birthday that afternoon. There was something about being close to all this that was doing it.

"An infomine," said Theo, and to Jules's surprise they could hear him.

"What's that?" Jules asked, but his words were lost in the din.

"You have to get your voice at the right pitch or I can't hear you," explained Theo. "An infomine. All information ever recorded anywhere is available right here. It's all zapping through here. The whole lot. You can find anything you want to know. All the answers are here. The trick is sorting out the question."

"What's everyone doing, then?" Jules tried a low voice and that seemed to work better.

"Exactly that. Trying to sort out the question," replied Franklin. "This is an inquiry into TimeJumping. Should the question be about Quincy, should it be about JumpMans themselves, or does the whole problem start somewhere else altogether?"

Franklin pointed out the speed debaters, who were rapidly thrashing out all of the arguments. There were issue searchers, random info dippers, lead chasers, deducers, deep-history searchers, unspinners, bias correctors, and many others whose roles were not so obvious.

As Jules watched further, he started to see the colored streams of light suddenly coalesce into pictures and text. Sometimes it might be a graph or a chart, or a document. Elsewhere footage would emerge or a piece of an audio recording would start playing. As he watched, he saw what looked like a picture of himself and Genevieve appear in front of some junior researchers, one of whom stared at it and then at them.

Then in the middle of it all, from a purple stream of info, a peculiar-looking man seemed to materialize. He was unblemished. He was neat and perfectly assembled. He seemed unnatural, striking yet kind of repellent at the same time. He began speaking in a grand manner as though he were making a speech in a huge hall.

Jules read the subtitles. BYGONES SUBMISSION TO INQUIRY INTO TIMEJUMPING.

Theo looked astonished. "The Bygones? They're just three old grannies who hate TimeJumping, aren't they?"

"Not anymore," muttered Franklin. He turned his attention to the speaker.

"Before the present crisis, how many of you were uncomfortable with TimeJumping anyway? Where were our kids going? What were they seeing? Kids as young as ten or twelve were Jumping off to watch blood-spattered battles, burning ships, bizarre religious rituals and ceremonies. It's one thing to go and see some saber-toothed tigers in their natural habitat, or perhaps the building of a castle. It's quite another to be Jumping in and watching those tigers tear a caveman apart, or watching while that castle burns and its residents die a horrible death."

"What is he on about?" said Theo.

A woman appeared and walked toward them. Two of the nanobots stood aside for her. She glided up to Franklin. She looked young, she looked old. She looked beautiful, she looked strange. She looked agitated and focused, she seemed calm and serene. It was hard to figure out how she was doing this, but she was all of those things at once and more. By her very casualness and her concentration, it was obvious she was in control.

"Franklin!" she said. "And our friends from Mil 3? Wip, who else would be wandering around with Franklin? Certainly no one from our time!" She laughed loudly at her own joke, and to everyone's amazement Franklin laughed as well. At least Jules decided it was a laugh. If it had been anyone else, you'd have rushed forward to try to stop him from choking. The other odd thing was that Franklin had gone a sickly shade of pink. He had a shy little smile on his face and seemed very pleased to see this cheerful woman.

"Walls! Get some seats for our friends."

Chairs formed in front of them, and Katherine leaned forward, touched one, and then giggled.

"Some juice and some nibbly things?" offered the woman. "I think so. Walls!"

The woman put out her hand and the walls delivered a tray of drinks and snacks to her.

The woman was kindly and smiled a lot and had one of those faces that could be somewhere between thirty and a hundred and ten. She had a smooth complexion but with an interesting line or two and a look in her eyes that suggested that behind the smiles and the pleasantries she had some deep experience, a lot of wisdom, and was not to be fooled with.

She handed around the drinks and then stood and addressed them in a compelling voice.

"Thanks for coming," she began. "My name is Mavis. Mavis Soap One. I'm prez of the Two Planets, which these days include the dust sifting factories of the moon, and of course the recently pioneered outposts on several of the larger asteroids. You are on Mars in the year Fourteen Billion and Seventy-three, which is about three thousand years ahead of your Mil 3. You are also illegal TimeIntruders, and we will have to decide whether to charge you with that or not."

She stopped.

"Franklin, I thought you said they were Oak-I with all this. You said they had to come here because they knew."

Franklin flushed a little more pink as soon as Mavis turned her soft brown eyes on him.

"The-The kids, Mavis," he stammered. "The kids know all about it. The parents have no idea."

Mavis sighed and rolled her eyes.

"No prelim? No contact? This is their first Jump? Well, they're in shock, aren't they?"

Tony spoke up. "Um, Mavis. Prez. Um. I'm sorry, but I'm not used to speaking up when I'm dreaming. I thought I was at parent-teacher night, but I'm not now, and if you could just wake me up, then I'm sure none of this will make sense but I'll be awake . . ." Tony trailed off.

Steven had a go. "We're on Mars? Mars? Mars, the planet?" Steven faded out.

Mavis smiled at them both.

"The accent, Franklin," she said. "It's pure Mil 3!"

Mavis drew back a little to address them all.

"This is an inquiry into TimeJumping. For reasons I hope Franklin will make clear, he has Jumped you all into the middle of it. It is true, it is real, it is simply to your eyes and minds unbelievable. But your kids have been doing it for months now."

Katherine clapped her hands together. "I knew it! Isn't this fun?"

"Hmm, fun?" said Mavis. "I don't know that it's fun. A lot of people are now very upset. Have you heard of Mr. Feynman? Leader of the Bygones? He's very angry."

The Bygones presentation was still going on: ". . . we've done the right thing by abandoning Earth. It's clear that we've evolved beyond Earth. It's a limited planet, limited by its own clumsy systems, easily corrupted, and it easily corrupts the humans who live there. Look at Quincy. Turns out all he was trying to do was line his own pockets. Typical Earth-like behavior: say one thing, do another.

"We should look only forward. We have created a powerful new civilization, and we don't need to go back to learn anything from the past. On Earth it's all too easy. Water falls from the sky. The air is always good.

Here on Mars to survive we have to think of every-thing, anticipate the slightest potential breakdown of our systems. When you don't know where your next breath is coming from, when the slightest miscalcula-tion can mean that everyone dies, then you really have to learn to work together. On Earth you don't have to care about anyone, and so who cares when no one cares?"

"See what I mean?" said Mavis. "Not happy. So let's get to it. We have a problem. I don't have any reason to keep TimeJumping going. Everyone's scared of it, and now we've got people like that banging on about it. Quincy corrupted the system. In fact, he probably was doing so from the very beginning. He never intended to maintain the past. He always wanted to change things to make himself more powerful. And the main obstacle to that was these two."

She pointed at Jules and Gen.

"These two grow up and have a profound influence on the future. We're not sure what they do, but we know it's something to do with everyone deciding to go to Mars. Quincy wants that to not happen. He wants to kill them."

Mavis looked both warm and grim.

"Jules?" said Tony. "This Jules? Are you sure?"

Jules felt like his dad could have been a bit more supportive.

"Quite sure," said Mavis. "Why? Do you think Theo Jumped there by accident in the first place? He was given a JumpMan of Quincy's with Gen's coords already in it."

"Who do they grow up to be?" Tony asked the question that was in everyone's mind.

"Couldn't tell you that even if I knew," replied Mavis. "Rule One: Don't Touch Anything. If they know what they're going to be, then they might try to not be what they're going to be, and that could undo the entire future."

Steven shook his head and began laughing. More than laughing. He stood up and he started screaming with laughter. He slapped his thighs; tears ran down his face.

"I'm sorry—," he started, and then he was off again.

A minute or two later he calmed down. "You know what this is?" He chortled. "Can't you figure it out?"

Steven gazed around at everyone, a greatly amused look on his face. "It's a show. We're on one of those shows!"

"What are you talking about?" asked Tony.

"It's one of those shows! We're going to have to live

here for months, right, and people will vote us off, or we'll have to meet every week and decide who goes back to Earth! Or they're filming us all, and at the end they tell us that it was all just a joke. It's *Interplanetary Survivor*!"

"I don't really know what you're talking about," said Mavis, "but this is no show. You're here, and you're going to have to stay here for a while. At least until we find Quincy."

The parents, of course, started to react to this. They crowded in around Mavis.

"Wait a minute—"

"We can't just stay—"

"Why are we here—"

Franklin, Theo, Jules, and Gen stepped back a little.

"You're never going to find Quincy, are you?" asked Gen.

Franklin shook his head.

"He still wants us, doesn't he?" asked Gen.

Franklin nodded his head.

"We're going TimeJumping, aren't we?" asked Jules.

The Bygones leader's speech was starting to crescendo and fill the room: "What has this focus on TimeJumping achieved? We would have left the solar system by now. Instead we have a whole generation looking inward and going off to play pirates. There are kids spending more time in the past than they are in the present. There are kids obsessed with following explorers or tribes or foods or music, and they've forgotten what Mars and the asteroids can offer.

"And worse. There are those doing it just for pleasure. For the thrill. That horrible recent development of Extreme TimeJumping: Jumping into earthquakes and volcanoes and tectonic plate shifts, and surfing tidal waves, and watching great beasts fight, or great wars unfold. This is a development in TimeJumping to be abhorred and resisted. We haven't come this far and worked this hard just to watch our kids turn into pleasure-seeking slobs, taking the planet for granted.

"And where does it lead? To a Quincy Carter One. A man obsessed with power and wealth. That's not the Martian way. On Mars we are rich when all are rich. We are rich when all survive. We can trust only when all are one and all are working to the one end.

"And can the TimeJumpers tell us where Quincy is now? No. And are Franklin and Duncan doing anything about that? Are they out there looking for him? Instead, they've gone to Mil 3 and brought two families to our time. Two Mil 3 families are wandering around loose here today. Excuse me, Franklin Nixon and Theo and all the rest of you. Rule One? Could you explain how bringing Jules and Gen and their parents here is in any way in keeping with Rule One? I don't think you can.

"This is too important to trust to those renegades and no-hopers. Suspend TimeJumping and arrest the intruders!"

Mavis smiled a sweet sad smile. "I can't stop him now. He's got the numbers," she said to them.

Things happened fast. The Nanobots closed in around them. Franklin grabbed Jules, Gen, and Theo and pushed hard against the nearest one, breaking them away from the larger group.

Gen looked back, and their parents and Cynthia suddenly seemed to be frozen in the middle of the room.

"Franklin, no!" she screamed as she saw Franklin reach for his JumpMan.

But Franklin ignored her. "ChronoCage!" he yelled. "ChronoCage! Nothing we can do for them. Come on, you three, we're out of here."

Franklin spun the dial on his JumpMan and pressed the GoButton.

They were gone.

THE PAST

MIDAFTERNOON, JUST BEFORE FULL MOON 13,000 BC

OLD TIME

"Why are you always twiddling with that rope, Two Brow?" asked Bug Lover as they walked over the hill to see the horses.

"You'll see," was all Two Brow said, twitching her eyebrows and smiling a little.

Bug Lover wished Star Speck was there so the two of them could exchange a meaningful glance about how strange Two Brow always was, but Star Speck had stopped coming to see the horses since he'd been spending all his days with Fleck. The horses did tend to bolt for the forest when they smelled the wolf, and these days Star Speck pretty much smelled like a wolf himself, so they found him a bit off-putting as well.

Two Brow they didn't mind, and Bug Lover had been there often enough for them not to worry too much about him, either.

One of them whinnied a little and trotted over to Two Brow.

As soon as he nuzzled forward to greet Two Brow, she held a piece of apple in one hand, and while the horse reached out to eat it, she slipped the rope over the horse's head. The rope settled over the horse's nose and he flipped his head a few times in annoyance but concentrated on the apple, and Two Brow was soon able to calm him down.

"What's that for? Why did you put the rope over its head?" asked Bug Lover.

"That's the trick. That's how I'm going to get on it. I'm going to let him get used to the rope. And then I'll use the rope to hold on to and I'll make him go where I want him to go."

"That's amazing!" said Bug Lover. "What in skies above makes you think that's going to work?"

Two Brow flashed a shy grin at Bug Lover. "I don't know. Gotta try. How's the vote for the wheel going?"

The wheel. *It was exhausting,* thought Bug Lover. He'd been to every hut, scrape, cave, rock shelter, and bit of bark leaning on a tree up and down the entire Long River. He'd never spoken to so many people in all of his days. And he'd never been so convinced that everyone was insane.

A typical meeting went like this:

Bug Lover: Hi, I've come to talk to you about the wheel.

Guy in Cave: Oh, yes.

BL: Do you like it?

GiC: I don't know.

BL: What's wrong with it?

GiC: I don't know.

BL: Is there anything about it that I could do better?

GiC: I don't know.

BL: Shall I put you down as a "don't know"?

GiC: I don't know.

"I have three like that every day," he told Two Brow. "And then I have three others that are terrified of it." Those meetings went like this:

Old Person in Rock Shelter: Why do we have to change? It's always change, change, change with you young people. You always think the new thing's going to be better.

Bug Lover: What new thing? There hasn't been any new thing since the fish hook. And Mugwamp the Storyteller thinks that was at least twenty generations ago.

OPiRS: Still, slow and steady grows the grass. All that loud music you listen to gets you overexcited. And then you think every new thing that comes along is going to be better.

BL: We don't even like music. Those guys using the mammoth horns, they're not us.

OPiRS: All I'm saying is, you've got to grind your corn to grist your grinder.

BL: I don't even know what that means. That's one of those things people say, like a stitch in time saves nine turtles. What does that mean?

OPiRS: It means we had our spear and our cutting stone and we were happy. We didn't have all the things you young fellas have. We had to make our own fun.

BL: Look—who invented the spear?

OPiRS: I don't know. We've always had the spear.

BL: Yes, but somebody must have made the first spear.

OPiRS: Well, that was a long time ago.

BL: And if it was, it still meant that someone had to sharpen a stone and tie it to a stick and say, "Look, I can throw this at that deer over there and it falls down dead and we can eat it." And I'm sure there was someone standing there who said, "It's too sharp. It's dangerous. What if you miss? We'll spend all our time making spears and we'll forget the old ways of jumping on deer, and we'll all starve and we've always lived without spears so why do we need them now?" I mean, I'm young. I make things like the wheel. You're old, you question it. That's your job. This is mine."

One old man had stood there looking at Bug Lover for a while. "You think you've got all the answers, don't you?" he said. "You young people always think you know it all."

"Oh, do what you like, you stupid old caterpillar!" And Bug Lover slammed out of the rock shelter, stubbing his toe on a grinding rock on the way.

And even those who liked it had the weirdest ideas about it.

Fan: Hi, Bug Lover. Love your new wheel. What colors does it come in?"

Bug Lover: Wood color?

F: Yeah, but couldn't you, like, decorate it, make it green or smear some great-looking orange ochre on it?

BL: I suppose.

F: That'd be cool.

Fan 2: You know what I want to do? Get one and paint, like, a tiger on it.

F1: Cool. I'm going to get one and paint a megarhino on it. Maybe put a big horn out the front.

F2: I'm going to hang a lion tail off the back of mine.

Bug Lover listened amazed.

BL: So you guys want to get a wheel, and then decorate it?

F1: Yeah, so it'll be, like, ours. Everyone'll say, "Cool set of wheels you've got there."

F2 : I reckon girls'll like it.

BL: What, if you've got a Wheel?

F2: Yeah, I reckon if you've got a wheel, they'll think

you're really cool. I mean, it's cool if you don't, but then you've got to be, like, a great hunter or gatherer or make great goats or something. But I reckon if you just have a wheel and you push it really hard and it's, like, red, they'll dig you.

F1: Red wheel, that's a cool idea. Why don't you make red wheels, Bug Lover? I'd give you, like, two goats for a red Wheel.

Bug Lover couldn't figure this out at all. He and Two Brow were still trying to make their wheels work in some way, and here were these guys who wanted one because they thought girls would like it.

"They like you, they like the wheel," said Two Brow. "Does it matter why?"

Bug Lover wasn't sure.

And then there were some who wanted more information.

Concerned Parent: Do you think it's safe?

Bug Lover: Sure.

CP: Have you done any tests?

BL: Tests?

CP: Tests. Seen if it hurts anyone, upsets any gods, causes rain or locust plagues?

BL: How would it do that?

CP: So you haven't tested it.

Pompous Self-Important Concerned Cave Dweller: Have you done any calculations about its effect on the economy? What are your figures?

BL: My figures? Why would it have any effect on the economy? What is the economy, anyway?

PSICCD: The economy, my young fan of bugs, is everything. You make us a fence, we give you a barbecued goat to take home for everyone. Someone else finds some great pears and exchanges them for some new skins. At the moment we're importing more mammoth meat than we're exporting. That's a problem. What effect will the wheel have on all of that?

BL [Shrugs]

PSICCD [Ignores shrug]: What if everyone gets a wheel and starts doing their own carrying? Mass unemployment in the carrying business. Will there be enough jobs in the wheel-making business to hire these people? Your notion that you're going to give them away—sounds dangerous to the economy. Better people pay for them, that way they think they're valuable. Give them away, they think it's a trick.

"I don't know," said Bug Lover in answer to Two Brow's original question about the vote. "I've spoken to everyone and I have no idea what they want, if they like it, or if they're going to eat me."

"Don't worry about it. They like it," said Two Brow, who didn't really care much about the wheel anymore. The horse she called Fella was nuzzling her armpit, and all she could think about was getting on his back. She felt as though she might try it in the next few days.

Back at the village Star Speck had said the same kind of thing. "It'll be fine. Everyone I talk to likes it." He was ignoring the fact that he hadn't really spoken to anyone since he'd been going everywhere with a wolf. People were scared of him. He'd been thinking of getting a new name for Fleck—not changing Fleck, but changing "wolf." Perhaps if he called her a sog? A bog? A dug? Something like that might make people feel more relaxed around her.

Bug Lover hoped his friends were right. There was nothing more he could do now anyway. Last night's moon was nearly full. The vote on the wheel was tonight.

chapter five
AT THIS POINT IN TIME

Blast was still pumping. It never closed. The machines were switched on and kids blasted away at the aliens and the enemy for months on end, until a piece of dust, a spark, a smudge on the program, brought the whole thing to a halt. Then the machine was bundled up and thrown out. A new one, brighter, faster, with bigger explosions and yet more levels, was brought in, switched on, and the kids went on blasting away at that one.

There were skinny Chinese boys in groups of four or five. There were kids in school uniforms. A few girls drifted in and out, but otherwise it was mainly boys and men. Men in suits after work, men who'd finished delivery shifts, some bike couriers, some builders off a big site over the road, they all gathered there to blast away, and get their adrenalin levels up punching the buttons.

It was a place where no one noticed anyone else. There was a kid handing out change and occasionally picking up rubbish. Some cleaners came through every morning before dawn. But no one paid any attention to who was there, when they got there, or when they left. The kind of people who went there weren't, at that moment, all that interested in other people. It wasn't conversation or society they sought. They were looking for action. They could play similar games at home, but these ones were bigger and faster, and the players could challenge themselves against the best on the street. So they walked in and looked around at the screens, at the machines, not at the people playing. They found the game they wanted, checked to see if their score had been bettered, threw some coins in, and fired it up.

And that's why no one noticed a short fat man with a gentle, almost jolly expression walk up the stairs, go to the third floor where the machines in Japanese and Korean were, and knock on the wall just behind an old Space Invaders machine left there as a living museum for players to laugh at. The short fat man waited for a moment until a door appeared, and then he opened it and walked through. There was the tiniest ripple and zap in the air as the door disappeared.

The short fat man was standing in a room without any decorations or furniture except for a chair and an odd-looking contraption behind it. He was dressed in big baggy shorts, expensive leather slip-ons, and a voluminous white shirt. Sunglasses and a neat flat hat finished off the ensemble. He was carrying some bags.

"You know, Feynman, I like the clothes. If there's one thing I like about Mil 3, it's the clothes. I like that you have to choose. They're already made and they don't change!"

Quincy Carter One put down his bags and pulled out a pair of three-quarter pants in a dusty khaki with some orange plastic toggles on the pockets.

"See? I saw these, and I thought, I like the little orange bits. And then I thought, I bet they don't have my size, but they did, and they were on sale!"

Feynman looked at Quincy and then down at his own pants, which were a simple pair of tan slacks. They changed instantly to exactly what Quincy was holding up with such glee.

"As usual, Quincy, you are entirely devoid of sense. We can make whatever we want, whenever we want it. All this entire era does is wrestle with crude chunks of matter and force them into unwieldy forms that take forever to break down. Everything they make ends up as garbage. It's insane, and you're loving it."

Feynman had almost no expression or tone other than a kind of permanent disdain. His voice, however, was beautiful, rich and seductive as a news broadcaster's.

"Yes, I know it makes no sense, Feynman," said Quincy, "but fun rarely does! And shopping is fun! I bet I had more fun buying these pants than you would getting the Nanobots to make you an entire wardrobe!"

Quincy did a little dance with his pants and then sat down to look at his other purchases.

Feynman turned away from Quincy, immediately removing the entire conversation from his memory as irrelevant, and returned to working on the odd contraption behind the chair.

Feynman was a strange-looking person. Very clean-featured, no trace of stubble, hair that sat just so, a nose, mouth, and eyes in perfect proportion. He was dazzlingly handsome, but when people looked at him, they felt distinctly uncomfortable. He looked so right, and that was the problem—he was too right. There was nothing wrong: no blemish, no spot, no pimple, no little hair or scar or dry patch. His skin was uniformly pale, from the orderly border of his hairline to the neat neck of his black

T-shirt. But what was most disconcerting was a sign of perfection that no one really noticed.

His face was perfectly symmetrical. Draw a line down the middle of his nose and his left and right sides were exactly the same. No one's face was like that. The left and right sides of everybody else's face were always quite distinct from each other. But then again, Feynman wasn't like anyone else.

Feynman wasn't human.

Feynman was a Nanobot. Or rather, Feynman was trillions of Nanobots operating together to form a single being.

Feynman was the result of the early Sixteenth-Billennium Nanobot system, which operated like an army. Each single atom-size Nanobot was part of a group of one hundred. Each group of one hundred had a slightly larger Nanobot in charge of it. Each group of one hundred slightly larger Nanobots had an even larger Nanobot in charge of it, and so on. Until you got to Feynman. Trillions upon trillions of controlling Nanobots made trillions of decisions per second to keep the structure and figure of Feynman walking around and operating in the real world.

Feynman was meant to be in charge of all the Nanobots. A kind of vice cheeo in human form who could communicate to Quincy and the others what was going on in TimeMaster's Nano Line, how the system might be improved, or what needed to be done if Quincy wanted something new. He was a liaison system and—almost as a joke, like so much of what Quincy did—he gave Feynman human shape.

"Oh, it makes things easier," he'd said at that time. "I can just yell at him, I don't have to program him! Besides, he's smarter than me, and I don't think I can say that about anyone else on the Two Planets."

In fact, Feynman was a lot smarter than Quincy. And he had none of Quincy's awkward little emotions and humors to get in the way.

Quincy pulled out some shoes. "See? Sure you can get the Nanos to make these, but I didn't even think of shoes like this! These are great." Quincy was holding up knee-high cowboy boots of blue and gold leather. "What do you think?"

Feynman barely glanced up from what he was doing. He just changed his own footwear to something similiar to Quincy's new boots, only longer, bigger, and brighter.

Quincy waved an impatient hand at him. "You just don't get it," he said. "Anyway, everything working? Another test? Or shall we go get Jules and Gen?"

Feynman turned and considered Quincy for a

moment. "Everything's working here. Pick your time, Jump in who you like, and do whatever you want. There is a small hitch, however."

"What hitch?"

"Jules. Oh, and Gen. They're not here. Not now and not on Earth."

Quincy went a dark crimson. He threw the boots across the room.

"My giddy clones! Where in the Two Planets are they?"

"Apt phrase, Quincy. They're on Mars."

"Mars?"

"Yip, Mars."

"They can't be on Mars. It's Mil 3. Mars isn't even inhabited yet. There's a couple of remote control cars sending back snapshots of sand—"

"Oh, I'm sorry, did I forget to mention it? They're also in Fourteen Billion and Seventy-three."

Quincy spluttered with rage while he looked suspiciously at Feynman. Had that pile of programming just been joking with him?

"How do you know all this?" he got out through clenched teeth.

"Instant reports from the Feynman 1.2 who is running the Bygones group. Have you forgotten you ordered me to make a double of myself and set about dismantling support for TimeJumping? Jules, Gen, and both their families are now on Mars. Taken there courtesy of our old friends, Franklin and Theo. This Feynman 1.1 is awaiting your orders. What are you going to do about it?"

Quincy paced up and down. Two Feynmans. He hadn't forgotten. He just wasn't aware of the kind of powers Feynman 1.1 had built into Feynman 1.2. He wondered if he was really giving orders to Feynman at all anymore.

"Something makes me think you've already done something about it," stated Quincy in a low steely voice.

"I have. I've locked the parents and a sibling in a ChronoCage in the infomine. Jules and Gen did manage to get away with Franklin and Theo."

"They've escaped!"

"Escaped? Would you call it that? I'm sure if we really want to find them we can."

Quincy circled the room, contemplating his next move and looking at Feynman suspiciously. Feynman had stopped even thinking about Quincy and was now taking his own head apart with a third arm that had suddenly sprouted from his left shoulder. Quincy didn't want to rely on Feynman quite so much, but now that he was here, he couldn't do without him. It was Feynman who'd built the new JumpMan in front of them here. It was through Feynman that Quincy could now change entire events and calculate the consequences. All he needed was Jules and Gen. Make them unhappen, and then Mars wouldn't happen, and then three thousand years of history was his to play with.

"Feynman. Could you do that a little more quietly?" Quincy asked. "You know, I think we should just get ourselves ready. They're coming. We ran the test on Jules's little friend. Jules will have told Franklin all about it. Someone's going to come and have a look. We just need to be ready. Either that, or they'll try to rescue their parents. We've got both covered. All we have to do is wait."

Feynman stopped working on his head. "And if they don't?"

Quincy let out a savage groan of frustration. "If they don't, then we will make it very plain to Franklin and Mavis and anyone else that we want them, and we will undo the past, the present, and the future until we get them!"

Feynman scratched the side of his head that he wasn't working on with one of his normal arms.

"And you think I can do all that?"

Quincy swung around. "Can't you?"

"Only joking. Of course I can." And Feynman resumed work on his own head with all three of his arms.

Quincy stared at him. He didn't remember programming a sense of humor into Feynman.

THE FUTURE
TUESDAY MORNING FOURTEEN BILLION AND
SEVENTY-THREE

Jules and Gen opened their eyes. Theo and Franklin were standing next to them. They'd Jumped, but Jules couldn't quite tell to where. Was this Earth, or Mars?

They were standing on top of a hill. Below them ran a river. It was wide and ran easily through its deep banks. Stretching away from the banks of the river as far they could see were the ruins of an ancient city. The ruins went to the horizon. The tall buildings were half-decayed and the streets were now overgrown with trees, but Gen had the impression that this must have been a significant and important city in its time. There was also something faintly familiar about it.

Jules looked around. Next to them on top of the hill were two or three decrepit brick and stone sheds. It seemed to be a rickety collection of old stables or storerooms, barely holding themselves together, like an old person pulling a worn cardigan around tired bones. In places it was hard to tell if there was an actual building there, or just a pile of used bricks stacked up waiting for a decent push to topple them over.

Attached to one corner of a shed was a short stubby tower with a rod pointing skyward on the top, and a rusty metal ball at the end of the rod.

Franklin pushed open a gate that screeched in protest, watched a startled armadillo waddle away, and yelled out, "Duncan!"

Jules and Theo followed him, but Gen stayed where she was and started yelling as well. "Franklin!"

When Franklin ignored her she got louder. "Franklin! FRANKLIN! *FRANKLIN!*" She stomped her feet and clenched her hands into fists. Theo grabbed Franklin by the coat and turned him around to face Gen, just as he was about to walk into the building.

"What?" he demanded.

"What WHAT? What's with you?" Gen yelled. "Every single time, you do it! Every single time. I can't believe it. You just Jump us anywhere you like without telling us anything. This time it wasn't enough to just Jump us to Mars in the future, now you've got my parents and Cynthia trapped or frozen or killed or something and you've jumped us AGAIN to . . . to . . . to wherever the hell this is!"

Franklin frowned and shook his head. "Your parents are safe. They are in a ChronoCage and locked out of time, but they're in no danger."

"It's like the first bit of a TimeJump," explained Theo eagerly. "It takes you out of the present and then just stops."

Gen stomped around a bit more, trying to disguise the angry tears that were starting up in her eyes. Crying really annoyed her.

Jules came over and put a hand on her shoulder. "It's started, Gen. We're Jumping again. We're going to have to see it through."

Franklin sighed and continued in a quiet, calm voice. "You are on Earth. This is called MeanTime. It's where the TimeKeeper lives. We need to see him because I think Quincy is behind the move to shut down TimeJumping. If Quincy is the only one left with access to the past, then who's going to stop him from whatever it is he wants to do? I thought you'd be safe here in our time. I'm sorry. But I don't think we have much time now. So if I'm going to save you, save the past, save everything, then you are going to have to trust me."

Franklin stood in front of Gen. "How about from now on you assume that I am a genius and know what I'm doing and you are a fourteen-year-old girl who hasn't a clue what's going on?"

Franklin didn't mean to sound patronizing, like he was talking to a naughty little girl, but he did, and it didn't do much to improve Gen's state of mind.

"I'm not some ditzy idiot, okay? You can't just decide everything for me."

Franklin put his face close to Gen.

"I so want to be sensitive to your needs. But when Quincy finds you, this time I think he might just dump the pair of you, and Theo as well for that matter, in the middle of a sulphurous sea and let the acids do their work."

Franklin turned and walked inside.

"I don't think he'll do that," said Theo.

"No. Not Quincy's style. Jump you under a guillotine as it's coming down, that's Quincy," added Jules, chuckling.

Both the boys laughed, and Gen went deep purple with anger.

"Oh, so now you're happy, Jules."

Jules looked suprised. "Yes, I am," he said as they followed Franklin into the building.

—

Jules knew he should be worried, but unlike Gen he felt strangely relaxed now that they were Jumping again. He'd been so nervous for weeks wondering if Franklin and Theo were about to turn up, wondering if Quincy was going to try to get them again. Now that it had started, he felt he could relax. They could maybe finish this thing. And in some ways, no matter how disastrous it was, it was exhilarating to be out here in the future. Maybe it would never happen again.

"MeanTime!" said Theo as they walked in through a tiny door. "Come on in and meet Duncan."

They walked through and into the room with the clocks. It was mayhem. Duncan was sweating and looking extremely nervous. Franklin was pacing.

"See?" Duncan was yelling. "The time ripple! I found it!"

He whirled around to see Theo coming in. He didn't seem to notice that new people had come in with Franklin and Theo. He kept yelling. "There was someone new at 1066. The Battle of Hastings. Someone Jumped and they killed someone who wasn't meant to die. Eight hundred and forty years later one of their descendants was meant to invent the can opener. See? No can opener! It's unhappened. The unhappening has started. Who are the children?"

Franklin introduced them.

"Blast!" Jules blurted out after Duncan nodded at them. "It's at Blast!"

"What?" asked Franklin.

"Max. He Jumped. He went to a battle somewhere and he killed someone. He called it a Jumper, or a TimeJump or something. We were at Blast, in Mil 3."

Franklin leaned forward, his eyes boring into Jules's.

"You're telling me now? You're only just telling me now?"

"I haven't had time to tell you before, and then I thought I was imagining it or going mad or something. I mean, it was the same with Theo. I wasn't sure if I was seeing him or not."

"You were seeing Theo?" screeched Franklin, turning to Theo. "You weren't even meant to be there. You were visible?"

"I was not!" protested Theo .

"No, he wasn't," agreed Jules. "I'd see him for hardly a second."

"Corner of your eye? Distracted? Confused?" demanded Franklin.

"Yes," said Jules.

Franklin grunted. "You slipped out of the present," he said to Jules. "Anyone can do it. You go into a room, can't remember why you went in, you've stepped out of the TimeFlow. All JumpMans do is keep you there. Whenever you were losing it, you slipped into Theo's time for a second, and there he was. Right?"

Jules nodded and then looked over at Theo, who had suddenly developed an intense interest in some of Duncan's gear, and then Jules looked at Gen, who had equally suddenly found her shoes fascinating. She looked up at him and mouthed, "Sorry!" Jules shrugged and smiled back.

Oh, nice work, said his brain. *Perfect. Couldn't have done better myself.*

What?

What you just did. You've won the argument, but then you just won the peace as well! Brilliant. She'll feel really bad for making you feel bad, and then she'll feel really good about how you didn't make her feel bad about making you feel bad. Excellent work, Jules.

Jules screwed up his face and banged the side of his head.

Brain, I don't need you.

I know, I know. But I still care.

Jules sighed. He had a sentimental brain. That was nice, he supposed.

He looked up to see Duncan staring at him intently.

"Things are starting to unhappen. Franklin, you go with the boy to this Blast. It's one unhappening. I can hold time in place for a while. Theo and the girl can keep Jumping to check Sites."

There was nothing to say. It was time to save time. They Jumped.

THE PRESENT
TUESDAY MORNING EARLY MIL 3

Jules opened his eyes and he was back in his own time, early Mil 3, outside Blast. Franklin was standing next to him. Or would have been if he weren't now leaping out of the way of a street cleaning truck that was spraying water all over him.

It was an odd sensation, Jumping into your own time like this, Jules noticed. It made his own time seem like a Jump site. He was observing everything, suddenly aware of things he'd never seen or heard before. He felt more like Theo as he noticed how everyone marched along the street with their heads down but still managed not to walk into each other. He noticed the incredible noise of the street. Cars, trucks, and buses were thundering by only a yard or two away from him, solid chunks of metal sucking at the air and at the ground, barely tamed beasts that could mount the pavement at any moment and crush him. They seemed more terrifying than dinosaurs.

It was hot, and the air was full of grit and dust. Bad smells wafted up from a grate in front of him. In every little corner there was a pile of chip packets, drink containers, and food wrappers. It was so noisy on this street. He'd always thought this was a great part of town, but now all he noticed was the huge building site over the road, with its clamoring jackhammers and drills and the blaring music coming from every shop on the row behind him. He wanted to get into Blast, where it might seem relatively peaceful.

Jules grabbed Franklin by the arm. "In there." He pointed. Franklin looked at Blast and his face fell.

"We have to go in there?" he asked.

Jules nodded.

Franklin sighed. "This is how you entertained yourself in Mil 3?"

Jules nodded again.

Franklin lifted up his shoulders, took a deep breath, and stepped forward into Blast. But he didn't get very far. A small man dressed in a green and black Blast uniform put a hand on Franklin's chest and said, "No. You go! Outside. No beggars! No losers! Outside!"

Not surprising, thought Jules. *Franklin does look more like someone in need of a handout than a guy who was one of the six brainiest people of his day.*

"What? Oh, I don't have time," snorted Franklin, and he quickly Jumped the man five minutes back into the past. There the man met himself coming in through the front door. He tried to stop himself coming in, and he got caught up in a fascinating tussle trying to throw himself out until he caught back up with the present and one of him disappeared again. He then retired to the food counter and spent the rest of the day counting chips.

By that stage Franklin and Jules had reached the top floor of Blast.

"Here," said Jules. "I was sitting here and Max came out of that corner over there."

Franklin frowned. There was nothing there except the old tabletop Space Invaders. And then his face cleared. There was nothing there. Everywhere else there was a game, a screen, a vending machine, a poster, something. This large blank stretch of wall seemed like a total extravagance in a space that was packed to the ceiling with machines designed to extract money from every passing player.

Franklin pulled back his sleeve to reveal his JumpMan. He keyed in a few codes and then pressed the GoButton. A doorway appeared in front of him.

"Oak-I," he said quietly. "A TSZ. Nice trick, Quincy, but not nice enough."

Then the door opened. Someone ran out, grabbed Jules, and ran back in again.

Franklin was so astonished at this rapid turn of events that he just stood there. And then as the door started to shut, he threw himself forward. The door slammed, and Franklin was trapped, half of him in Blast, half of him on the other side of the door. He screamed more in surprise than in pain.

The man who'd snatched Jules looked up.

It was the same man who'd been leading the Bygones on Mars. He was now placing Jules in a chair and arranging a ringlike attachment above his head.

Standing next to them and chuckling with deep amusement was Quincy.

"See, see! They did turn up! I knew they would!"

"Quincy!" roared Franklin. "Open the door. This is insane!"

"Insane? You want insane? Get a mirror, Franklin!"

"Time to stop now, Quincy. You've made your point. Oww." The door squeezed a little harder on Franklin, although no one was pushing it.

"Made my point? Made my point? You think this is a debate, Franklin?"

Quincy came up close, and Franklin could see the madness in his eyes and feel his breath—intense and sharp—on his face.

"I'm not making a point, Franklin. I am the point!"

"Why? Why, Quincy? What is the big deal?"

Quincy shook his head sadly and stepped away from Franklin.

"You never got it, did you? None of you did. Duncan, Mavis—you never got it, you never saw what we had. You wanted to look but not touch. You wanted to find some old statues and some books. You wanted to see who we were. You know what I wanted?" Quincy's voice tightened again into an intense powerful stab. "I wanted to see who we could be! What we might become!"

"You mean what you could be. This is all about you!"

"So? If I could change history, eliminate the mistakes, the mess, the time wasting—imagine what humanity might become. History is so slow to get going! Great Genomes, Franklin—how long does it take for some caveman to figure out that it's easier to keep a goat on a rope than it is to try to chase one every second day? I mean, even if they did it twenty thousand years earlier, think where we'd be now. Imagine if it had happened one hundred thousand years earlier. We could be across the galaxies!"

Quincy was roving the room. Behind him Franklin could see Jules twitching and turning, and then he disappeared.

"Jules!" he yelled out.

"Ah, got it working then, Feynman? Excellent. Few short test Jumps first, and then we'll get serious. Want me to stop, old Franks, you crazy old electrode? Bring me Genevieve as well, and I'll see how I feel."

"Stop what, you megalomaniac? What are you doing now?"

"We've downloaded a little JumpMan chip into him. And then once he's out there on a Site or two, he's just going to interact a little with the locals. Should be interesting! Ever seen an unhappening?"

Quincy came back across the room and got up close to Franklin again. "I'll stop anytime you bring me the girl. Got the boy now. Bring me the girl, and we're done. Otherwise, I might just see what this little baby can do!"

"But why? What is it with them—oww!"

"Oh, I'm sorry, Franklin. Bit uncomfortable being neither here nor there? We're nowhen inside here. Out there, Mil 3. You're in both. Must be uncomfortable."

Franklin was starting to feel like he might split in half, but he didn't want to show Quincy that. He was about to yell at Quincy some more, but on his Blast side he could feel someone pulling on his arm, trying to get his attention.

"Sir? Excuse me, sir. Are you all right?"

With the eye that was in Blast, he saw two men in blue uniforms. One of them was talking into a radio and summoning more "units," whatever they were, into the vicinity. The other was trying to get a response from him.

"Sir, what happened here? What seems to be the problem? Is this door jammed in some way?"

Franklin would have liked to explain that, yes, the door was jammed, but it was jammed between their ongoing TimeFlow here in Mil 3 and the TSZ—temporal suspension zone—that Quincy had created here, a space that floats apart from time like a plane in a holding pattern.

Franklin could be removed from the door, but he would have to be physically torn in half. Half of his body left in the TSZ, the other half lying on the floor in Blast.

"No!" he yelled out the side of his mouth that was in Blast. "No, I'm fine. Go away! Leave me alone!"

The two men in blue looked at each other. The one

on the radio spoke again. "Update on George Street Blast situation. We'll need psych help, ambulance, and fire. It's a 724."

Franklin paused and then laughed. "Yeah. Tell 'em to throw in the straitjacket. I don't know if the injection will be enough."

"Sir?" the other officer said. "Sir, we're going to need your help. Can you open this door, or are you caught in some way—"

"GO AWAY. What if I like it like this? Yip, that's it. I like it. This is why I come here. I stick myself in the doorway. Now leave me alone. It's my thing. It's what I do. So go away."

"Got a little problem back in Mil 3 there, Franklin?" said Quincy. "Not a lot of choices here at the moment. You could come in all the way. Or I could move the TSZ and tear you in half, or . . . I know—you could tell me where Gen is and that would finish the whole thing."

Quincy smiled brightly at Franklin as though he'd just invited him over for tea and scones.

"Thanks, but I'm sure I'll figure something out. Quincy, what is it with Mil 3 and you? What is it with Jules and Gen? Why are they so important?"

"Ah, now we get to it." Quincy threw his head back and assumed a kind of lecturing position. "Franklin, haven't you realized that sometimes it's not the big important obvious thing that matters? Usually the big stuff was going to happen anyway. Sometimes it's one other little moment, someone, somewhere, just at the right time, who just gives something a little push, or just makes a little invention, or says the right thing, and that's what makes all the difference."

"Jules and Gen?"

"Jules and Gen. Crucial. Without them Mars doesn't happen."

"The evacuations?"

"The evacuations—that marvelous moment when the rich get so rich they take over the entire planet and need somewhere to send everyone else. So they develop Mars—and then get richer again."

"You don't want to develop Mars?"

"I don't want them to develop Mars. I want everyone to stay on Earth so that I can develop Mars!"

"But I know the history of the evac, and the founding of Mars. Jules Santorini, Gen Corrigan—what did they do?"

"Sir?" The two officers in blue were tapping on Franklin's shoulder again. "Sir, the ambulance people are here now. Along with the fire patrol. We'll have you out of there just as soon as we can."

"Hello? Can you hear me all right?" Franklin squinted out of the eye that was in Blast.

"No one's going to make you do anything you don't want to do," said the nice policeman.

"Then go away and leave me alone. I have to stay here. You don't understand. Behind that door is a man who wants to undo history and throw it all away. Leave me alone. Go away."

A pleasant-looking woman stood back and conferred with the police, who withdrew and started setting up tape and pushing everyone back. The firemen continued to move some tools and gear into position.

"Is there anyone we can contact for you?"

"SHUT UP AND STOP TALKING TO ME!"

"You're getting very agitated there, Franklin. What are they doing to you in Mil 3?"

Behind Quincy, Jules flickered back into view, groaning and moaning a little in the chair.

"Jules is back. Isn't that nice?" said Quincy.

"But not for long," said Feynman, and off Jules went again.

"He's done a good job, Franklin. You should start to see some results quite soon. Your little charge, I can see why you've wasted so much time on him. He's very quick and resourceful. And very, very obedient. Anyway, nice being here to catch up. Time you either came in or got out of here, quite frankly. Got a few things to do, and I'm sure you can always find something to amuse here in Mil 3. Go buy some clothes, they're fabulous! Bye!"

The TSZ started to dissolve. For a split second Franklin felt the door give way. He threw himself back into Blast and knocked over the waiting psychologist.

She picked herself up and then turned to Franklin. "So you're feeling much better then, sir? You decided to come out of the door?"

"What door?" said Franklin.

They turned to see that where there had once been a door there was now a smooth blank wall. While they stared, Franklin whipped his sleeve back, activated his JumpMan, and was gone, leaving two police officers, an ambulance driver, two firemen, and a psychologist with a lot of explaining and many months of counseling ahead of them.

INSIDE THE TSZ
NO TIME

Although it seemed to Franklin as though Jules had been snatched away suddenly, for Jules the whole thing had happened in slow motion. He'd walked quietly into the Room, and there had been Quincy. Alongside him was a nice-looking man who looked exactly the same as the nice-looking man who'd been so angry about TimeJumping a few minutes ago on Mars. Was that only a few minutes ago? He'd been to Mars, to Earth, and now back to his own time in about half an hour? It wasn't just being inside the TSZ that was giving Jules a distorted sense of time.

Jules walked past a fly that seemed to be stationary, but then he noticed a slow downward movement of its wing.

"Hello, Jules." Quincy waved. "Nice to see you again!"

Jules felt very odd. He knew that Quincy wanted to kill him and Gen. But somehow in here he felt like Quincy was his friend. Like an uncle he'd always trusted.

"Temporal indifference," the nice-looking man said, pointing at the fly. "Time is all about how you relate to it. In a TSZ there are no minutes or seconds or hours. There is only now. And whichever now we decide should come next. It's easier if you keep a bit of order, but not essential. It's slightly unsettling at first, but you'll get used to it soon enough, Jules."

Jules nodded. The nice man took his arm and guided him onto the machine in the middle of the room.

"Take a seat," the man said, and his voice was smooth and flowing like a cheery TV voice-over.

The seat felt very comfortable, and Jules was fascinated to see the glowing ring that the nice man was arranging above his head. The ring descended. Jules felt a tiny burst of pain inside his head and then nothing.

"You've TimeJumped, Jules?" the man asked.

"Oh, yes," replied Jules, "quite a few times, actually."

Jules was feeling very dreamy. Not asleep, but as though he were now in a dream. He wasn't outside of himself, he felt perfectly normal, but he was speaking like he was a character in an English book. The nice man was smiling kindly at him, and Jules felt that everything was just super.

"Am I going to TimeJump now?"

"Yes, you are, you lucky boy," said the man.

"Oh, goodie," said Jules. "Do I get a JumpMan?"

"You are a JumpMan!" replied the man.

"Super!" said Jules. "Where am I going?"

"Everywhere!" said the man.

"Splendid!" said Jules. And he closed his eyes.

He opened them again quickly.

"Invisible?" he asked.

"Nip! Visible. We want everyone to see you!"

Jules closed his eyes once more and Jumped.

When he opened them again, he was on the moon. He knew it was the moon because the Earth was rising just like it does in those classic photographs of the Earth taken from the moon back when astronauts first went there, in the last years of Mil 2. The earth was green and blue and covered with swirling clouds. It rose into infinite blackness, and looked stunningly beautiful.

Jules looked around at the grey landscape of the moon. Jagged mountains everywhere, and thick moon dust under his feet. His feet! Look at those shoes! Big white clumpy shoes, connected to big white bulky pants and the rest of what must be a space suit. He felt around his head and there it was, a space helmet. He could hear himself breathing.

In front of him was a small landing craft, not much bigger than a car, with spindly legs and antennas and dishes on the top. A ladder was descending. It bit into the moon's dirt, raising a dust cloud that, without any atmosphere, fell straight back onto the ground.

A door opened in the side of the landing craft. Two legs appeared, dressed in the same kind of suit that Jules was wearing.

Jules's radio crackled into life.

"Houston, Tranquility Base here. CZZKKSK. The

Eagle has landed CSCCCSZCSC." Each phrase was punctuated by a stab of static.

Jules watched fascinated as the figure descended the ladder to the moon's surface. The radio crackled into life again.

"That's one small step for man CXCZCZCX. One giant leap for mankind—oh, hang on, Houston CXCZ-CXCZCX. We've got a problem. CZXCZCZCXC."

"Go ahead, Eagle. What's the problem?"

"There's someone already here CZXCZCZCX."

Jules waved.

Neil Armstrong waved back. And then he tapped Buzz Aldrin on the shoulder and pointed in the direction of Jules.

Jules waved again. And then disappeared.

Jules opened his eyes. He was back in the TSZ, staring up into the face of the nice man. Everything seemed tweaked up a little. The colors were a little brighter than they should have been, the sound was both intense and far off. The man's face loomed into focus and seemed too large when he was up close, and then seemed to be a long way away as he withdrew. But Jules felt happy. Like a little boy. He didn't have to think about anything. He was making no decisions. Feynman was in charge. Where and whenever he went, Feynman could tell him what to do.

From far off and quite near at hand he heard voices.

"Well? What happened?" demanded Quincy.

"Perfect. I send him whenever I like, he does whatever I want. See?" replied Feynman, pointing at a console not unlike the ones attached to the games on the floors below them in Blast. "We've just been to the moon landing. July 1969, in Old Time. Only when they got there, they found they weren't the first. Jules was already there!"

"That should make a mess of the next few years for everyone," chortled Quincy. "Sure Duncan will pick that up?"

"Someone already on the moon? Makes all sorts of things unhappen."

"Got any more, Feynman?"

"Got a a few I want to do for fun. May I?"

"Don't let me stop you!" urged Quincy. "Just get the message through to Franklin. Send me Gen, or look what I can do to the past!"

Jules opened his eyes again. He was standing on a city street. But it was nothing like George Street or any street in his town or time. It looked like something from an old movie. Big steel cars with fins rolled by like slow-moving sharks. Pickup trucks backfired as they parked. Some women strolled by wearing big dresses, curled-up hair, and pointy sunglasses. Two men leaned against a wall, shirtsleeves rolled up, smoking cigarettes. *The 1950s,* thought Jules. *This is the 1950s.*

He looked around him. He was standing in front of a store. He read the sign painted on the window.

SUN STUDIOS

RECORDINGS OF MEMPHIS'S FINEST

DO-YOUR-OWN-DEMO!

JUST $10!!!!

PROPRIETOR: SAM PHILLIPS

He turned around to see a young man climbing down from the driver's seat of a truck. The young man glanced at himself in the side mirror and pushed his hair back into place. He was handsome, and swaggered as he walked toward Jules. He stopped and pulled out a pack of cigarettes, shook one free, and lit it. He drew on it deeply, read the sign in the window, turned around, and went back to his truck. He leaned against the door, and then pushed himself off and started back toward Jules. He went up and down the street a few times.

"Can I help you?" asked Jules as the young man sauntered nervously past him one more time.

"Well, kid, I can't rightly see how you could." The young man spoke in a thick drawl, but with a warm smile. His blue eyes were quite compelling. Jules liked him immediately.

"You've been up and down here six times," said Jules. "What's the problem? Sometimes it helps just to talk to a stranger."

Sometimes it helps just to talk to a stranger? Jules's brain pushed through all of a sudden. *What are you doing? Don't you realize who that is? When you are?*

But as quickly as his brain had resurfaced, it was gone again. Jules was back in his floating happy state, Feynman firmly in control.

"Well, ain't you just the doctor," the young man said, but he stopped, let out a lungful of smoke, and pushed his hands back through his hair.

"Name's Presley," he said. "Elvis Presley. Pleased to meet you, sir."

He was polite and put out his hand for Jules to shake.

"Santorini. Jules Santorini," said Jules, shaking Elvis's hand.

"I been telling myself for weeks now, I gotta go into Sam's studio and cut myself a demo or I'm gonna be driving trucks the rest of my life. Now I'm here, I just can't do it."

Jules nodded. "Turn around. Get back in your truck and thank your lucky stars you ran into me," said Jules.

"Excuse me?"

"I'm going to let you in on a little secret, Elvis. I'm not from around these parts."

"You ain't kiddin'. Kids round here don't talk like you none," said Elvis.

"No," said Jules. "I'm from the future. And I'll prove it in about thirty seconds, because I'm going to disappear. Right in front of your eyes."

Elvis's face crinkled up a little at this.

"I know, I know," said Jules. "You're thinking, This kid's as cracked as catfish with a crawdad in its craw-belly, right?"

Elvis's expression changed to amazement. "You know, that's exactly what I was thinking! How'd you know that?"

"Doesn't matter. I did, and like I said, I am going to do you a big favor. You're thinking of cutting a little number for your dear momma, and you thought you might do—"

"Why, you must be from the devil himself!" exclaimed Elvis. He looked deeply troubled now. "How you know all that?"

"Turn around, Elvis. I'm from the future. In a few

189

years from now, music is dead. They try this rock and roll thing—"

"Rock and roll?"

"Rock and roll—and everyone hates it. The only music they like in the future is the piano accordion."

"The pee-anner accordion?"

"The pee-anner accordion," confirmed Jules. "So unless you want to go and cut a polka or two this afternoon, or some Italian love songs, or a little gypsy jazz, I'd get back in my truck, drive on out of here, and go buy Momma a nice new housedress instead of cutting her some songs she ain't gonna be proud of just a few years from now."

Jules was starting to sound a little like Elvis.

"I gotta go, Elvis. Remember, I knew what you were thinking, and look—I can just disappear!"

And he did.

Elvis leapt back like something had attacked him. He looked around, but no one seemed to have noticed anything. He ran a hand through his hair and considered the door of Sam Phillips's Sun Studio one more time. Then he shook his head.

"Thank you," he said, looking up at the sky. "Thank you very much."

And he walked over to his truck, threw it into reverse, and drove away.

Jules opened his eyes. He could hear laughter.

"You got Jules to stop Elvis from making his first ever recording?"

Quincy broke up again into laughter. "Feynman, can you get serious?"

"I hate Elvis!" chortled Feynman. "And now he has left the building. Forever!"

"I hate opera, but I don't need you to go and upset Mozart. Do you think you can do something that matters?"

"Sure, sure," laughed Feynman. "Watch this. See here? Look, you can see what's going on, on the little screen."

"That's amazing quality!" said Quincy.

"Isn't it?" said Feynman. "And you can choose different angles. Take a look from Jules's POV!"

"Wow!" said Quincy.

But Jules didn't hear that bit. He was already floating high above the earth, looking down through some wisps of cloud at a bare windswept field below. He could see two figures pushing what looked like a large kite into position.

He swooped a little lower.

Jules. You don't have to do this.

A part of Jules swam back into his mind. He didn't have to do this, did he? Why was he doing this?

Go with that, Jules. Trust me. I can get us out of here.

Oh, that's right. It was his brain. The dreamy, happy, floaty Jules who was having so much fun pushed the brain away and brought his attention back to the past that was now present in front of him.

Below him the two men were turning the flimsy machine around. They both stood back and looked at it for a moment, and then one of them climbed into a precarious seat in the middle of this jumble of timber and wire.

Jules realized what he was looking at from several different school projects. It was the Wright brothers. And they were about to take off on the world's first ever powered flight. The invention of the airplane was about to occur just below him. A short hop of a few seconds, but enough to convince them that they could go a bit farther next time.

Jules was suddenly struck by the fact that he was looking down at them. He was flying.

Flight hadn't been invented yet, but he was flying. He was piloting a tiny little craft with a nearly silent motor behind him and some slick-looking wings that swept back like a fighter jet. By moving a stick around just in front of him, he was able to swoop and turn and bank and climb like he was a migrating goose. Not that he was in control of this flight. It was Feynman who was in control of him.

Don't! screamed his brain.

It was weird the way his brain was back with him. Yelling at him. Suddenly popping up. Apart from that, Jules felt all excited like a giddy kid at a fairground. This was better than TimeJumping with Theo. This was really wild. He felt perfectly safe and he didn't have to decide anything! Feynman was doing it all.

Jules swooped down until he was flying only a few yards above the ground. He swept in along the world's first airstrip at Kitty Hawk. He was close enough as he made his first pass by their craft to see Orville Wright's face go into shock. He could see confusion all over Wilbur's.

Jules laughed, climbed steeply, turned, and swept back down. He barrelled straight at them. At the last moment he pulled up and swept over the top of them, just missing the plane by a few inches.

He watched the brothers look at each other in astonishment. He saw Orville climb out of the seat and run with his brother after Jules as he pulled away.

Again Jules turned and came down toward the strip. This time he landed. Smoothly and easily.

He grinned at the brothers as they came closer. Then he gunned his slick little ultralight and took off, climbing steeply into the sun.

A few seconds later he was gone, leaving behind him two brothers walking sadly back to their shed. Someone else had got there first and slipped off gravity's leash. Their great dream lay shattered. Why bother now? The two brothers slumped down in their shed, contemplating a long and dull future of bicycle repair.

"Oh, that was very good, Feynman," Quincy said, and laughed. "What does it do?"

"Just messes up the whole chronology of the discovery of flight."

"Do you think they're getting this back at MeanTime?"

"Yes," said Feynman. "But why don't we send them something they can't miss."

"Let's send a message," said Quincy. "This should let Franklin know I'm serious. I want the girl. If he brings her here, I'll stop making everything unhappen. Have you got anything that might focus his attention?"

"Try this," said Feynman.

FUTURE NOW
TUESDAY MORNING FOURTEEN BILLION AND
SEVENTY-THREE

After Franklin and Jules Jumped, Duncan stared for a while at Gen and Theo. Gen stared back and then decided to ask a question.

"How do you hold time here?"

"Love to tell you, but that's just so the wrong question. See, if you'd asked something like this: 'Given that the Earth as it moves in orbit can deviate by up to one degree each solar cycle, how do you allow for that in your calculations of time,' then we could talk. But—"

Gen snorted. "Well, thanks, Duncan. Glad you want us to help."

Duncan looked at them and shrugged. And then an insistent beep started from a screen just above his head. He frowned.

"Another ripple. More unhappenings. Unboid, unboid."

Gen and Theo had come up and were peering over his shoulder.

"Get away!" Duncan snarled at them. "You got anything to offer, let's hear it. Otherwise, get out of here!"

Gen and Theo scuttled out and back into the

courtyard. They wandered over to the edge of the hill, sat down, and looked at the view.

"MeanTime," said Gen thoughtfully. "There's a thing called Greenwich mean time in Mil 3. I think it's a place. Is this Greenwich?"

Theo shook his head. "I don't know," he said quietly.

They sat awkwardly for a moment or two.

"Theo—"

"Gen—"

They started together.

More awkwardness.

"Theo, why were you Jumping into school?" asked Gen.

"Ah. I'd pitched the whole Mil 3 school idea as a JumpSite and needed to check out the best SitePoints, ideal coords placement . . ." Theo trailed off. He didn't sound that convincing.

"I always hated Mil 3," he said after a while. "We all did. It was stupid. It was the time when everyone got greedy. Well, not everyone. Just those people who could. They took everything. And then they kept on taking and forced everyone else to go to Mars. For three thousand years since, we've hated Mil 3."

Theo looked out over the river and the town. His hair was all natural streaks of wheat and gold. His coat had gone quite rustic, the kind of thing you'd wear for a walk on a brisk autumn day in the country. Gen thought he looked almost normal and calm.

"And then I get stuck with you guys and we go to school, and well, I'd never seen anything like it. Your schools are wild. Everyone is just off doing their own thing, everyone talks, there's so much action going on and none of it's in the class. And you've got friends!" Theo's face lit up. "That's a great idea. I've got two study buddies and some TimeJumping partners, but nothing like you guys have friends. You hang out after school, you talk all through school, it's the only reason you go to school."

"Oh, that's a bit much. We go to school for school, really."

"Nip, you don't really. If there were only those classes at school, every kid would be sick every day. It's your friends you go for. For lunchtime and after school. That's just great."

Theo fell silent. It didn't happen in Fourteen Billion and Seventy-three. After a learning session you got back in your pod and were home in minutes. Everyone stayed in their homes and got the walls to do everything for them. Create conversations, link them up with other kids. Or if he went out, he could TimeJump, SolarBlade, or do all sorts of amazing things. But there was not the same kind of intimacy and even freedom that a kid in Mil 3 had.

"And I really like you, Gen." Theo spoke so quietly, Gen wasn't sure he'd even said it.

"Oh," she said, feeling as though she should say or do something but not entirely sure what that should be.

"WHAT ARE THOSE MOON CLONES DOING?"

They both leapt up, startled. They could hear Duncan yelling and swearing back inside the tower. The mood was broken, and they ran in to see what was happening.

Beeps were going off on at least three screens.

"I'm holding July 1969, February 1954, and December 1903, and there's more coming! It's all unhappening! Go! Go!" yelled Duncan.

"Go where?"

"Pick a date. If it starts beeping, Jump there! Try and stop it!"

Gen and Theo looked at a screen and, sure enough, the alarm went off.

Theo grabbed Gen by the hand, and they Jumped.

chapter six

SAVING TIME

Jules was starting to giggle. A tiny part of him, somewhere on the left side of his brain way at the back, felt like he had nothing to giggle about at all, but he couldn't help it. Whenever Feynman brought him back, he and Quincy would be laughing their heads off, and Jules, still under Feynman's control, still in a strange almost hypnotized state, couldn't help himself. He was doing some pretty funny stuff. In quick succession they did a great run of uninventing.

Alexander Graham Bell had been a cracker. He'd been sitting in a small brown room thinking about what you might call his latest invention. It was a telegraphic voice converter and amplifier. He'd been calling it the televoxamptranaphone, but he'd noticed that his assistants couldn't really remember that, so he was trying to find something else. The transelemicimpulifier. The electrorepulseindicurorator. Needed to be catchier. The magnovox. The talking letter. The summoner. What did his assistants shorten it to? The televox? The teletran? And just as he was about to remember, his invention rang.

Alexander Graham Bell was more than a little startled. He'd forgotten that he'd attached a bell to it, so that frightened him a little. But even more shocking was the fact that he'd only made one of the devices so far. So who could be calling?

He picked up the handset, placed it to his ear. He could hear some chatter.

"Two large? Three? No anchovies on the supreme? And a large ValarJuice. Hello?"

"Hello?" said Alexander Graham Bell.

"Home delivery, please," the voice said. "Could we get two large pepperoni, and three large supreme, hold the anchovies? Large ValarJuice."

"I beg your pardon, who is this speaking?"

"Who are you? Is that Domino's? What number have I called?"

"Number?"

"Yeah, what phone number is that?"

"What do you mean?"

"Sorry, pal, don't worry about it. Wrong number."

The line went dead.

Alexander Graham Bell sat for many minutes with the handset up to his ear, waiting to hear more.

Nothing happened. Wrong number? What did that mean?

He sat for a long time looking at his invention. Then he calmly leaned down into his tool kit, picked up his strongest hammer, and brought it crashing down on top of the first phone, smashing it to pieces. He swept the pieces up and threw them on the fire.

And then he turned his attention to some drawings he'd been making. *Forget the phone,* he thought. *My electric sock-darning machine—that's the way of the future!*

Quincy laughed and slapped Jules on the back when he returned from that one. "Edison," he yelled. "Go make Edison uninvent the electric lightbulb, will you!"

In Edison's lab, filaments were lined up in neat rows, attached to electric cables. Some of them were burning strongly, some sputtered like candle stubs in the rain. Jules came in holding a birthday cake with six lightbulbs on top of it.

"Happy birthday to you." he sang. Thomas Edison and his assistants looked up, puzzled. Was it someone's birthday?

"Happy birthday to you, happy birthday, dear Tommy, happy birthday to you."

Jules finished on a big note, put the electrified cake down in front of Thomas Edison, and said, "There you go, Tom, now blow out the bulbs and make a wish!"

Thomas Edison looked at Jules. "You can't blow out the bulbs!"

"Exactly! Glad you realized it. Now how do you think people are going to feel when they can't blow out the bulbs? We've had candles for centuries. You think we want to give them up?"

Edison looked worried.

"People love candles. Who's ever heard of a bulb-lit dinner? What do you light when you need a romantic mood? Seventy-five watts of pearl? Uh-uh. Let me tell you, these lightbulbs can't hold a candle to—a candle!" Jules finished off with a fine flourish.

Edison slapped his hand against his head. "What have I been thinking?"

"You haven't been thinking, Tom," said Jules. "Look at all the know-how and gumption and plain old fangwangelry you've wasted on this stupid thing. You know what I'd do?"

"What?"

"Make candles that stay alight for days, months, even years."

"By jingo, that's a capital idea!" exclaimed Edison. "The Edison Eternal Flame."

"I love it, Tom. The Edison Eternal Flame—it's brilliant. Electricity: It'll never last, it's a phase, a fad. Stick with what the people love! Give 'em more of what they want! You can do it. Burn that candle at both ends, and I know you'll crack it!"

When Jules disappeared, Edison's assistants threw all of the glass, filaments, and wires into the garbage, then gathered around and watched a candle burn, looking for the secret to making Edison's Eternal Flame.

"Feynman, are you doing all this?" asked Quincy.

"You know, Quince," said Feynman, wiping some tears from his eyes, "I'm not. I'm giving Jules some guidelines, but he's doing the rest."

"He's good, isn't he?"

"He's very good. Shall we do a biggie?"

"You mean really big? Bigger than phones?"

"Let's show 'em what we've got!"

THE PAST

THURSDAY AFTERNOON 1685 OLD TIME

Gen and Theo Jumped. When Gen opened her eyes, it took her a while to figure out what she was looking at and why it looked all wrong. She was standing on a lawn, and around her were some largish stone buildings. She didn't know where they were, but the buildings were of the type you might find in an old university or large school. They were a few stories high, and they were long, with rows of windows, and they were built around a quadrangle of lawn and garden. Arched corridors of stone stretched from one building to another, and they echoed with the sharp footfalls of scurrying students and teachers. Everyone was wearing flowing black robes and strange hats, and as she watched them, Gen suddenly realized what was odd about this scene. It was all new.

These were the kind of buildings that in Mil 3 were three or four hundred years old. These were brand spanking new. The stone was smooth and clean, the mortar white and fresh. In the middle of the quadrangle was a small young sapling. The lawn was new, one or two young ivy plants were beginning to send a shoot or two up the walls, everything was even, neat, and like it had been finished yesterday. The fountains worked, some gardeners were preparing a plot with new rose bushes, other workmen were putting in a sundial.

Nothing had begun to discolor or fade or sag. The steps were not worn; the pathways weren't rickety and uneven. And like a new building today, these halls and classrooms and lecture theatres stood out, blunt and ugly, still to find their place and settle into the surrounding fields.

Theo grabbed Gen by the arm. "Cambridge University, 1685," he said. "Great place if you want to study Greek. Or hang out with Isaac Newton."

Theo took her hand. "Come on, let's go find the orchard. It's round the back."

Round the back they went and soon found a small orchard of about fifty apple trees. Stretched out underneath one tree was a youngish man, perhaps in his midtwenties. He was wearing a shirt with a big ruffle on the front, pants that were tied up at his knees, and below that white stockings and black leather shoes with big silver buckles. He had long hair tied back in a ponytail and was reading and muttering to himself.

"Damn them. Damn them! Could it be any simpler? For everything that happens, something else has got to happen. For every action there's an opposite reaction that's the same. But then I read here in Revelations that the horsemen will arrive on clouds of thunder, breathing fire and billowing smoke. Well, I am forced to ask, Perchance, how can a horse breathe fire? How can something living create something that would burn it? Are there laws of nature, or are there laws of God? If God can just do what he wants when he wants, then there are no laws? Or did God make laws that I am meant to see? Why have laws if our Lord can just fool around with them whenever he feels like it? What would the source of the fire be in our fire-breathing horse?"

Gen watched as a servant approached with a message.

"What? Go away! Tell them I don't care if I never see them! And don't come out here ever again!"

The man scowled at the servant, became absorbed in watching clouds go by, and then returned to his reading and muttering.

"There he is," said Theo.

"That's Newton?"

Theo nodded. "He's not pleasant," he observed. "Everyone has an equal and opposite reaction to him."

Gen had to agree. She didn't really know who Isaac Newton was, just that he was a very famous scientist who had done something very important, and that she was meant to know who he was. *Famous scientists,* she thought, *should be making grand discoveries in laboratories full of bubbling beakers. Not sulking under apple trees and being nasty to the staff.*

"It's not the most riveting Jump site in the entire history of the world," continued Theo, "but it's a pretty important moment. Newton discovers gravity."

Gravity. That's what it was, thought Gen. She knew he'd done something important.

"Without gravity, well, there's not much else, really. I mean, you can forget about flying to Mars for a start," said Theo. "So even though it's not that packed with action, we all come here at least once. You watch the apple fall and hit Newton on the head, and then you watch him scowl and mutter, 'Why didn't that apple fall up? Why didn't that apple fall up? Why didn't that apple fall up?' He just keeps on saying it over and over, and then after a while he starts to say, 'Everything falls down. Everything falls down. Everything falls down. Feathers. Snow. Rocks, trees, and maybe even the stars above fall down. Why? Why? Why? Why shouldn't something fall up?'"

Theo was going to talk more about this crabby little man who was in fact one of the great geniuses of all time, and Gen would have been interested to hear more—it's not every day you find yourself at one of the turning points of history, is it?—but then they both noticed someone walking toward Newton. Someone who was not meant to be there. Someone who had never been part of the story, but someone who was there now.

It was Jules.

In the TSZ Jules had opened his mouth to ask Feynman and Quincy what kind of big unhappening they had in mind, but before he could get the question out, he was no longer in the room with them. He was standing in an orchard on a bright, clear, sunny day.

He could smell the fallen fruit rotting on the ground. He could hear the buzz of bees. It was a very nice day. A beautiful day to change the course of history, really. On the other side of the orchard, sprawled under a tree, he caught sight of a man. He was lying on the ground, had some books around him, and was sighing and muttering to himself.

Jules looked up at the tree the man was lying under. There it was. And all he had to do was climb the tree.

Don't climb the tree.

Oh, brain. You're no fun.

This is not fun. You don't have to do this.

Jules felt a slight sensation of discomfort, something pricking the bubbles of excitement. *Why wouldn't I do this?* he thought. *The sun is shining, the birds are twittering, and all I'm doing is playing a little joke. A little rearrangement of the order of events. What harm could it do?*

All he was going to do was pick one apple. And there was the one to pick. The one hanging on the branch directly above the man's head. The one that looked like it might fall off at any moment. Wouldn't it be terrible if it fell off and hit the man on the head? *See,* thought Jules, *I'm doing good here, I'm preventing an accident.*

Below him the man was still muttering away, sometimes reading, and then bursting into more mutterings and questions.

Jules climbed the tree, reached out, and picked the apple. He climbed back down the tree, and as he walked away through the orchard, he shined the apple on his shirt and then took a bite. It was delicious—sweet, juicy, and firm. Best apple he'd ever tasted. He smiled and then the field of hay disappeared and he was back with Quincy and Feynman.

"Did I say you could eat the artifacts?" Quincy said, chuckling, as he swiped the apple and took a bite himself.

Jules smiled at him. "It's good, though, isn't it?"

"It's very good, Jules. It's very, very good!"

Gen and Theo had watched as Jules climbed the tree, took the apple, walked away, bit into the apple, and then disappeared. They turned and spluttered at one another.

"It was Jules—"

"It was Jules, wasn't it—"

"What was he—"

"He took the—"

"Where's he—"

"What should—"

And then they stopped. Newton was getting up. He slammed his books shut in disgust. "Bah!" they heard him yell. "Science! Logic! Laws!" He shook his fist at the sky. "Alchemy is where the answers are! I'm going to change metal into gold. Just watch me!" And with that he stomped off across the fields.

Gen's and Theo's eyes widened. At the same time, they reached for the JumpMan and pressed the GoButton.

They arrived back at MeanTime to find Duncan bent over some screens, looking intense and worried.

THE FUTURE
TUESDAY AFTERNOON FOURTEEN BILLION AND
SEVENTY-THREE

Gen and Theo spluttered some more at Duncan.

"Jules took the apple—"

"It was Jules—"

"And then he disappeared—"

"Is he back?"

"What's going on?"

Duncan slowly turned around to look at them. Gen wanted to ask about his skin care regime. She'd started to figure out that he must be at least as old as Franklin, but he looked so good. He was frowning a little now, however.

"Jules? You couldn't stop him?"

"Stop him? How would we—"

"You've got to stop him. Newton has just decided not to discover gravity. How many ripples do you think we'll get from that? Do you really think I can contain that? I'm reaching breaking point here, you know. Nothing is infinite, and that includes the capacity of MeanTime to keep all these events out of the flow of history. I let them go, we could all unhappen!"

Theo and Gen felt like little kids who'd been really naughty. Duncan started to proclaim: "We are in the midst of a mass unhappening. Time ripples are flowing like tidal waves through history. Soon events will start to run backward. Humans will be unborn. Whole societies and epochs and eras will simply never happen. Other events and eras will happen in their place, but who knows what they'll be like?"

"Just because an apple didn't fall?" said Gen.

"Rule One," said Duncan, shaking his head. "Maybe it's not Newton and the apple. Maybe it's just moving a piece of furniture. Look at your own short life. If you'd turned left instead of right one day, you might have walked under a bus. Or you might have found a cure for cancer. Who knows? The entire structure of human history is an endless series of choices. Who knows which are the ones that matter? We all knew that when we got TimeJumping going. But Quincy always thought he could beat it."

Franklin suddenly arrived in their midst.

"Quincy and some guy who looks exactly the same as the guy on Mars are holding Jules. They seem to be sending him places—"

"Isaac Newton's orchard," Duncan said, and brought Franklin up to speed.

"Great asteroids—you didn't try to stop him?"

"How do you want us to stop him? Wrestle him, throw spears at him? What exactly do you think we should do?" said Theo. "How come you lost Jules, anyway?"

"Quincy's not stopping, you know!" yelled Duncan. "He's going to keep on going until he gets what he wants."

Gen felt Duncan's eyes burning into her. It went very quiet.

"Someone has to say it," continued Duncan. "I like you, Gen. But are you worth the collapse of history, of all time? The moment I can't hold these events out, the moment Quincy's unhappenings hit the flow of history, we wash away millions of people. Everything that's happened is now in danger."

Duncan stopped speaking. Even the clocks seemed to have stopped.

Duncan was right, thought Gen. *I'm one person. What does it matter what happens to me?*

"Jump me to Blast," she said quietly.

"No way!" yelled Theo. "That's not right either!"

"How long can you hold it all in place?" Franklin asked.

"How long is a stream of protons?" replied Duncan. "Which stone will shift the star? When is enough enough? How—"

"ALL RIGHT," yelled Franklin. "I get it! You two, Jump. Try to catch Jules. Do anything you can to disrupt him. Everything you stop them doing is one less thing we have to worry about here. We'll do what we can. GO!"

They Jumped.

INSIDE THE TSZ

NO TIME

Jules was going fast now. He was Jumping in and making major historic moments unhappen in a few minutes. He convinced Queen Isabella of Spain not to bother sending Columbus in search of the Indies, because the world was really flat; he met with a group of Arab scholars close to discovering the number zero and told them not to bother as it would all add up to nothing. He chatted to some nice chaps in the islands of Indonesia about to float in some canoes to Australia, and told them about sharks. He persuaded some lovely men in China that all fireworks did was scare people. Gen and Theo missed him every time.

In Vienna, in 1807 Old Time, Jules arrived on a narrow cobblestoned street and stood outside a tiny house. He could hear a piano being thumped, and through the window he caught sight of a man, with a stern expression and a great mane of silver hair, staring down at the keys and then back up at the ceiling.

"Duh duh duh daaa," he sang, and then repeated the phrase a little lower. "Duh duh duh daaa."

Beethoven, thought Jules. *I've seen him on coffee cups. And that's his Fifth,* he thought.

Not the Fifth, said his brain.

Why not the Fifth?

Jules. Stop. Don't go up. Work with me. It's me. I'm you. Quincy wants to hurt you. To hurt Gen.

Jules stopped for a moment. Gen. Where was she? *She'd love this,* he thought as he ran up the stairs two at a time.

Ludwig van Beethoven crouched over the piano and thundered out the opening notes of his Fifth Symphony. He caught sight of Jules and broke off.

"Wo is du?" he asked, because he spoke German. Jules was amazed he could understand him. That JumpMan chip was pretty powerful.

"Jules Santorini, Lou—"

"Get out!"

"Sure, but before I go can I just say this—that opening phrase?"

"Yes?"

Jules made a face and held his nose between his fingers. "It stinks," said Jules, shaking his head and screwing up his face.

"It does?"

"You can't start like that."

"I can't?"

"Nooo! Try this—Daaa daaa daaaa duh! Not three

short and then a long. Three long and then a short. Much better!"

"You think?"

"I do!"

Beethoven tried it out.

"Sorry, Lou."

"Yes?"

"Not those chords. Keep it up."

"Up?"

"It's too dark. People go out, they want something up!"

"They do?"

"Sure! Something they can dance to. That first thing: downer!"

"Downer?"

"Jah! Downer. Anyway, sorry to interrupt. Must have got the wrong place. Auf Wiedersehen!"

Beethoven barely looked up.

The strange little boy had been right. Perhaps he was too moody. Why not write something "up"? He felt a lot of tension drain from his shoulders. He'd been thinking about his symphony for months. Now his fingers picked out a light little tune, his right hand joined in with a jolly oompahpah accompaniment, and he chuckled to himself.

His neighbor looked up from making strudel. *That's*

more like it, Herr Beethoven, she thought. Much better than his usual morbid thumping.

That afternoon Beethoven reeled off jolly little ditty after jolly little ditty, only stopping when two more strange children appeared next to his piano asking about Jules.

"Gone!" he shouted, and rattled off another pleasant little air, which, like his other efforts that afternoon, was hugely popular in its day and then promptly forgotten.

Jules arrived back in the TSZ humming. Feynman smiled broadly.

"That's music finished! Go get literature, kiddo!" Quincy said, laughing.

Jules had a sensation of enormous fun. He was giddy and giggling. Mere TimeJumping was boring. *Why just go look when you could do this?* he thought. It was like he was playing, or really more like he was being played. Each time he went to a new historical period, it was as if he were entering a new level of a video game. He was just the figure on the screen. Feynman was the player. He was the one making the decisions and determining everything. Jules simply went along with what he was being told.

It's not fun, his brain yelled at him. *Gen. Think about her. Don't you want to help her?*

Jules felt his giddy sense of fun evaporate. Suddenly he didn't feel quite so jubilant.

That's it, Jules. Feel miserable, urged his brain. *You're doing terrible things!*

But they feel so good.

Doesn't make it right.

The chip inside Jules's head reasserted itself and threw his brain out. Jules took a moment to remember where he was.

London, 1603.

He ran through the open doors of the Globe Theatre and into a dressing room, and slapped William Shakespeare on the back!

"Will, old son, how goes the play?"

Shakespeare looked up. "The play goes as it goeth, and at the moment it goeth not. Are you here to audition?"

"Um, ah, yes!" Jules was surprised at his response. Here to audition? That didn't feel right. He was here to mess things up, surely.

"You're young. Some rouge and paint, you might work. Okay, try this. You are a young girl of the Capulet family. About to turn fourteen. You've just clapped eyes on the Montagu boy, Romeo, and Cupid has emptied his mischievous quiver into your heart. Your families, however, are sworn enemies. Juliet is on a balcony, and she speaks. Go to!"

Jules took the pages from Shakespeare.

"O Romeo, Romeo—"

"You're a girl, boy! Has your voice broken?"

Jules nodded.

"I need innocent youth to play a maiden, not a rough calloused lad!" Shakespeare sighed. "Try once more. Light voice, swooning girl, you know the thing."

"Wherefore art thou, Romeo?" continued Jules. "Deny thy father and refuse thy name; / Or, if thou wilt not, be but sworn my love, / And I'll no longer be a Capulet."

Love. This is love. This is like Gen!

Jules looked at Shakespeare, who was staring at him with a pained expression on his face.

"What's in a name?" Jules stumbled on. "That which we call a rose / By any other name would smell as sweet; / So Romeo would, were he not Romeo call'd, / Retain that dear perfection he owes / Without that title. Romeo, doff thy name—"

"God's bodkin," thundered Shakespeare. "Stop now, lest I to Sirens make and demand they stop my ears with wax!"

"I'm sorry—"

"Sorry? Sorry is if you trip on a word. You have murdered my lines. Slain them in a manner most foul. I wouldn't cast you to carry a spear. Get out! What now?"

Shakespeare's angry gaze snapped toward the door.

Gen and Theo were just coming in.

"Jules!" yelled Gen.

It's her, yelled his brain. *Juliet! Be Romeo—*

"Gen?" said Jules. "Wherefore art thou—"

And then he disappeared right in front of them.

"What madness happens here? Where did he go? What do you two want? Tell that fool who pretends to produce to leave me alone. Stop sending me these waifs in monstrous garb. Does he want a play or not?"

Theo and Gen backed out and returned to Mean-Time.

They slumped down against a brick wall.

"It's not working. We can't stop him. Give me the JumpMan," demanded Gen.

"Nip! Nip way." Theo shook his head and clutched the JumpMan firmly to himself. "Get back, Gen."

"Just give it to me, Theo. This is crazy. Millions of people are going to die. The whole world is going to be turned inside out, and I can stop it right now. Don't you think I should?"

"Nip, I don't!" yelled Theo. "You go there, he's going to do it all anyway."

Gen calmed down a little. Theo moved toward her.

She leapt and wrestled him to the ground, grabbing onto the JumpMan.

"Give it to me! Let go, Theo!"

A wiry hand grabbed the back of her top and hauled her up.

"It's Jules we want you to go and wrestle. Not each other," said Franklin, glaring at them. "And you know what? I'd say this is the last Jump. Either get him this time, and don't let him muck things up, or we're all finished anyway. Oak-I?"

Franklin seemed almost cheerful, if a touch brittle. He gave them a funny little wave.

"Jump, children, Jump!" he ordered. "Got to go back inside and keep my finger in the dyke!"

Theo looked puzzled at that one. Gen nodded. They Jumped.

Jules felt decidedly unwell. He was back in the TSZ, but the whole giddy joy of everything had evaporated. He felt like a kid at a birthday party who's had a great day stuffing himself with cake and now wants to vomit everywhere.

Quincy and Feynman were leaning over him.

"What happened?" demanded Quincy. "Shakespeare

threw you out? You were on a roll. What happened? Feynman, check the chip."

The ring descended around Jules's head.

Feynman shrugged. "It's working."

"Give me replay," demanded Quincy, moving round to look at the monitor.

Jules felt a strange tugging sensation in his head. There was a whirring in his ears, and then it stopped, backed up a bit, and things calmed down.

"There! Who's he looking at? It's them! They're chasing him! Gen and Theo. Excellent!"

Quincy and Feynman came back into his vision.

"Off you go. Go play tag with your friends. And let them win, Oak-I?"

Gen and Theo opened their eyes. They were in a hot dusty valley. A stand of trees was a little way off. They were around two million years back in time.

Up in one of the trees were three or four creatures that looked a little like underfed monkeys. Gen and Theo walked slowly toward Jules, trying not to alert him to their presence or scare the monkeys in the tree.

The monkeys were really horrible-looking. They had skinny scrawny little arms and legs and short bloated torsos. Their heads were pointy and ugly, with teeth that were brown and green stumps. Raw bleeding patches of skin showed through their fur. They scratched at themselves and each other. They screeched and bared their teeth and fought constantly.

Even from this distance Gen could smell a raw scent coming off them—somewhere between a sickly sweet smell of biscuits baking and food rotting in a Dumpster. It wafted at them like pollution. The four creatures skittered neurotically around the trees, picking at leaves and tearing at the bark.

Jules stood calmly underneath, watching them.

It was hot, and it was dry. Withered-looking plants were everywhere. Patches of grass hung on like the last bits of hair on a bald man, and everything seemed cooked in this heat-blasted landscape.

"Jules?" said Gen.

Jules turned at the sound of her voice and looked surprised, but then he quickly turned back and ignored her.

"Jules, what are you doing?"

Again Jules turned, half-smiled, and then returned his attention to the apes.

"Jules, it's me and Theo! What are you doing?"

Jules acted like he hadn't heard anything, and started to circle the tree.

"It's not him," said Theo.

"What?"

"Wip, it is him, but someone's controlling him. He's not doing any of this. Quincy or someone with Quincy is. He's on the end of the remote, and he just has to do what he's told!"

"What's he trying to do? What are we doing here?"

Theo pointed up into the tree.

"See that nasty-looking ape up at the top there? The one with the black teeth, the scabs on her tongue, and virtually no hair on her legs?"

Theo was pointing at a really disgusting-looking monkey. It had a bad temper and was screeching over and over at the other monkeys.

"Take a look at your DNA, darling—first monkey down from the trees."

"That one? But it's horrible."

"Don't say that about Grandma. She might be horrible, but she's the only one with the guts to come on down."

Gen looked doubtfully up at the monkey, who was now scratching herself raw with one hand and picking things out of her hair with the other. Whatever she found she immediately ate.

"That's our ancestor?"

"Yip. Lot to be proud of there, you know. Plenty of initiative, daring, and ingenuity. Lots of get-up-and-go. The others are just too frightened. She comes down from the trees, scampers over the hill, and finds a water hole. You should see her in a couple of weeks. She looks terrific. She leaves them, wanders around for a while, finds a male who's nearly dead, and persuades him to come exploring. They walk on a bit farther and find an oasis, a spring. Water pouring out of the ground, lots of plants, birdlife, plenty to eat. They couldn't be happier.

"All the other apes stay in the tree, and they die. These two have babies every year for the next twenty, all of them scampering about the place and eventually heading out to find other spots to live, and before you know it, a few million years have gone by and there's good old us."

"Adam and Eve," said Gen in a hushed, awed tone.

"I don't know their names," said Theo. "I would have said her name was Oonk and his name was Onk, but you can call 'em what you like—I don't think they're going to answer."

"So, what's Jules going to do?"

"Wip, I'd say he's going to try and keep our scabby little friend in the tree."

The nasty-looking monkey had come down to a

lower branch on one side of the tree. She was ignoring the others, and was now eyeing the ground.

Jules moved around and stood underneath her. He looked her in the eye, and then said, "Boooo!"

The monkey looked astonished and bared her teeth.

"What are you doing?" yelled Jules. "Go back! Go on, get back up in the tree, you big hairy ape!"

Gen thought calling a big hairy ape a big hairy ape was probably not much of an insult. Like calling Jules a medium-size smooth-skinned human, but she had to admit the sudden utterance of human speech two million years before it would be developed did have the desired effect. The ape scuttled back up into the tree and clung to its trunk.

"Come on. Let's get him," yelled Theo, and he and Gen ran forward and grabbed Jules. They flung him to the ground and held him down.

Jules smiled at them.

"Hi, Gen. Hi, Theo. Come with me! It's fun." And then he grabbed them both by the arms and held them tight.

They all disappeared.

They were in a room. A room with smooth walls and little else. They were still hanging on to Jules.

"Genevieve. How nice to see you again."

Gen went cold. It was Quincy.

She turned around and he was standing next to a man who looked exactly the same as the guy on Mars who'd been making the speeches about TimeJumping.

"The Bygones?" she said, pointing at Feynman.

"Aren't you clever?" said Quincy. "In fact, as far as I know, the United Planets are about to send the TimeCops in to pick up old Franklin and Duncan, and that should about be that. Hello, Theo."

Theo glared at Quincy. He was too upset to speak.

"Where now?" asked Jules in a faint voice. "Wherefore now? Whatfore next?"

"Feynman? Did you analyze the long-term effects of having a JumpMan chip in the middle of your head?"

"Nip," replied Feynman. "Jules is the first."

"I think it really starts to affect them. Jules has gone quite strange. Shall we?"

Feynman stepped forward and grabbed Theo and Gen in an inescapable grip. They both felt a tiny moment of searing pain and then nothing.

"Chips installed!" said Feynman.

"Let's all go, shall we?" Quincy said, and then chuckled, and everyone Jumped from the TSZ.

☺

"Where are they?" shouted Franklin when Gen and Theo failed to return to MeanTime, and a sweating, pale Duncan shouted back at him, "I don't know. They stopped Jules that time, though. But we're done here. I can't hold anything more back. They eat a banana that's not meant to be eaten, and we're finished. It'll all flow. It'll all go."

Something blinked and went out on the masses of screens in front of them.

"The TSZ. It's closed."

An insistent beep started up from the other side of the room.

"Not there," said Franklin. "They haven't gone there."

Duncan looked up.

"Quincy's got them. And, yes, they've gone to where it all begins!"

Duncan nodded. "You go. It's hopeless, but try to stop them."

Franklin Jumped.

chapter seven
NOT BEFORE TIME

THE PAST
WINTER, FULL MOON 13,000 BC OLD TIME

Quincy, Feynman, Gen, Theo, and Jules all stood in a clearing by the Long River. Jules had a half-crazy smile on his face. He looked over at Gen and Theo, who smiled dreamily back at him. It had them too. A giggly bubble of excitement made them feel lightheaded and silly, like nothing really mattered.

"Hey!" yelled Jules. "Come on in. This is Time-Jumping!"

Gen laughed.

Theo punched him on the arm.

"Now you're teaching me how to do it, Dodoboy?"

Quincy looked at all three of them. "Well, look at us all. Haven't we been a long way together? You know, this is all your own fault. You, Gen and Jules. All your fault. You had to interfere. You had to go and rescue Theo when he Jumped into your bedroom. You had to get involved. You could have just let him go. You could have ignored him. But you had to go TimeJumping. And you, Jules—you had to go and get a glimpse of the future. Which means, of course, that you become the people I don't want you to be. Oh yes, a lot of the future rests on you two. And that future happens because of what you did when Theo was in your present."

Jules, Gen, and Theo weren't really listening to Quincy. They could hear him off in the distance, but Gen and Theo were lying down in the grass giggling, and Jules was standing near them, swaying and looking insane.

"I could tell you everything, but you're not hearing it. And what does it matter now? I've tried to just undo your little actions and get rid of at least one of you when I could. But you had to go and get Gen from Pompeii. You had to go and find Franklin. So now, I've got to go right back and change it all. Change history completely. Just so it suits me. All right, Feynman. Let's finish up here. Haven't we learned a lot chasing this little guy around? Chips working?"

Feynman nodded.

"Right place?"

"Long River," replied Feynman.

"Right time?"

"Late fourteenth billennium, or around 13,000 BC Old Time."

"Excellent. The beginning of it all!" Quincy bent over Gen and Theo and yelled in their faces.

"You Mil 3 people think you've got to deal with change. Computers and cell phones? That's nothing. This lot is about to go from half a million years of snatching squirrels and grubbing for nuts to having horses, the wheel, and the dog, in about three generations. Place is exploding with change."

He smiled deeply and looked into Jules's eyes. "But not enough for me. Kind of handy having you three here. Gen, just up ahead you'll find a nice young boy called Star Speck. He's got a dog. Make the dog go away.

"Theo, over that hill the Stug family tradition continues. Do what you like, but keep them off the horse.

"When you're done, come and find me and Jules, and then we'll all get rid of the wheel. Any questions? No? Okay, enjoy!"

Gen went over the hill, and there was a boy about her age playing with a dog that was somewhere between a puppy and an adult. Everything was slightly the wrong size—the head a bit big for the body, the feet too big for the legs. It was lolloping clumsily around the boy, who was laughing as it leapt about trying to grab something from his hand.

She watched for a while and then ran down to join in.

"Hi!" she yelled merrily, and got the dog's attention.

She snatched the bone out of the young boy's hand and ran off toward the end of the clearing. The boy looked shocked.

"Don't worry about it," she called back.

There was a faint sense deep in her stomach that she was doing something very wrong, but it was faint and distant and way below the overwhelming feeling that this was fine and fun and she was having a great time.

The boy stood watching her go, not quite believing what was happening to him. Then he started crying and rushed into a hut.

Gen ran into the forest, the big puppy dog lolloping along behind her.

"Come on," she called. "Here's your bone. Come and get it!"

The dog was right on her heels as they ran deeper into the forest, jumping over fallen trees, dodging around thickets of thorny-looking vines, leaping small streams. The dog seemed to be enjoying itself, and Gen, whose idea of exercise was to roll her eyes upward at the very mention of it, was surprised at her own stamina. She could barely walk to school, but here she was running like a sleek young hunter through the forest, twisting and turning, up and down small ridges and gullies, the dog happily tracking her all the way.

She ran a bit farther, and then the dog ran up past her.

"Hey," she shouted, but the dog didn't return.

Breathing a little bit heavily, she slowed to a walk. Then she stopped altogether.

She could sense rather than see eyes watching her. She slowly turned around, and just when she thought maybe she was imagining the whole thing, she saw something. A glint of yellow brown.

And then another.

And then a hint of silver, and then a larger version of the dog she'd chased off trotted into view and stood looking straight at her. Behind her she heard panting, and she turned around to see another, and then three more arrived.

They were wolves. They were not menacing her, but they were surrounding her, so despite her giggly euphoria, she did feel a little threatened. The first one was still standing staring at her, but every now and then its eyes flicked away to acknowledge that a few more had come to join them. Gen dared to look around for a moment. Now there were twelve, maybe fifteen wolves in the clearing. They'd formed a circle and all were standing, leaning forward, unblinking. Except for the first one, which had now sat back on its haunches. It had been joined by the dog Gen had lured away.

Not that it was really a dog, as in a cocker spaniel or a red setter. It was a young wolf cub, Gen now realized.

The wolf cub lay down with its head up and watched as the circle of wolves closed in on Gen.

She yelled. She jumped up and down and waved her arms about. The wolves didn't care. They stopped for a moment but then, like a disciplined army, padded forward as one, until Gen was hemmed in tight by bigger, leaner, tougher versions of the cute puppy she'd first seen only minutes ago.

Gen could hear them panting, clouds of breath coming from their glistening mouths. She could hear some of them growling low, and one or two barked.

And then, just as she was wondering if this was it, if the wolves were going to encircle her but not do anything, over the back of the pack came the lead wolf, the wolf who'd been sitting out of the circle with the cub. It leapt high in the air, paws out, and landed right on her chest, knocking her flat to the ground. The wolf stared into Gen's eyes for a moment, snarled deeply, and lifted its head. Its jaws opened wide and its head lunged down at her face.

Gen screamed, but nothing seemed to come out. She tossed her head from side to side, waiting for the crunch of bone, for the sound of teeth tearing her cheek off, for what she imagined would be unbearable pain.

She opened one eye cautiously. Instead of a slavering wolf head in front of her, all she could see was gray sky and the towering trees of the ridgetop.

Then Feynman's head came into view.

Gen giggled. "Bit close there!"

"Yes, sorry about that," said Feynman. "Got a bit distracted. You got rid of the dog, though?"

"Yes, looks like it's gone back to the pack."

"Excellent!" said Quincy. "Hate dogs. Dogs gave man big ideas. They crawled into his camp, licked his hand, and became his friend. Suddenly man thought, well, why not the horse? Or the goat? What if I could tame the lion? Get rid of the dog and man feels alone. He doesn't feel his special power over the animals. He keeps thinking he is an animal. Besides, I'm a cat person. I've never liked dogs. And one thing I always said was that when I get things sorted out, I'm going to bring back the cat. I hate all those damn armadillos."

Theo ran back over the hill and joined them.

"How did it go?"

"Easy!" he replied, snapping his fingers. "I just kept Jumping in and out in front of the horse, and that kid went straight off the back of it. None of them could see me, but the horse could sure smell me. Freaked him right out, and he's still galloping away. I don't think anyone from that family is ever going to try that trick again."

"Oh, you're such good children," said Quincy. "Shall we finish the wheel?"

"Yaaay!" they all cried, and ran off over the ridge.

Bug Lover and Moon Smacked stood next to each other in the clearing at the bottom of the Meeting Hill. The moon was full, and they both shone silver in its light.

The tribes were excited. Bug Lover could feel the tension, the anticipation in the air. There'd never been anything like this before. Moon Smacked had dubbed it a voat, but Bug Lover had suggested it was more like a vote, and Moon Smacked had shrugged and said, "Oy Ka," and so all members of the tribes of the Long River were now gathered on the Meeting Hill for the vote on the wheel.

Moon Smacked spoke first, "Elders, witch doctors, tribesmen, almost-sentient Primates, and those yet to be impressed by their opposable thumbs, welcome. I think I have spoken to you all in this last moon, and what I have noticed as I have gone into your huts and your caves, your scrapes and your shelters; as I have sipped far too much rotting leaf litter and tongue thickener; as I have shared your grasshoppers, your pig knuckles, and your wheat cakes so tasty with crushed grubs or flower stems; what I have noticed is that you lack for nothing. You are happy, you are fed, you are safe. Each year the hunt goes off and returns with meat and skins for us all. The Long River brings us fish. The wheat grows high, and there is fruit from the trees for everyone. What can this wheel bring us, except harm, trouble, and pain?"

Moon Smacked was very moving, and all were silent as they gazed at him. Some nodded along. A few leaned toward their neighbors and asked them to explain what was going on, but they were quickly hushed up.

"I say no to the wheel. Not for me, not for you, but for them—"

And from the shadows, Moon Smacked brought forward two young children of about five and six. One had an adorable bone through his nose, the other long blond hair and a lovely leopard skin draped over one shoulder. Their noses were clean, the grease wiped from their hair. They smiled shyly up at their uncle Moon Smacked.

"Do it for the children. For their children's children. Why risk anything when it is not you or I who will pay, but them who will know the suffering, the weakness, the terror that comes in the wake of anything new like this wheel."

Bug Lover, Two Brow, and Star Speck looked at one another and shook their heads. Could Moon Smacked go any lower? This was such a cheap trick. Surely the tribes wouldn't buy it. *But there you go,* Bug Lover thought as he looked at them. *They're wiping their eyes, a few are nodding, and a few more are banging their hands together in approval.* Well, it was up to him now.

Bug Lover stepped forward into the moonlight. "First, friends, don't forget. We vote, and whoever has the most on their side, that's what is going to happen. I've seen you all, and I know that deep in your hearts you're excited about the wheel. Don't let Moon Smacked scare you. There's nothing to be afraid of. Except to know that I may not be the only one to think of the wheel. The tribes of the Long Valley, the tribes of the High Mountain, the tribes of the Far Desert—they all log roll, don't they? So maybe one of them will think of the wheel. And maybe they'll use the wheel against those tribes who don't have the wheel. There'll be a wheel race, and I say we can't afford to lose that."

Bug Lover didn't like to use this argument, but he felt there was some truth to it. The thing about the wheel was that he never felt like he'd invented it—more like it was just waiting there for him to notice. To see that this thing was possible and then to see all the things it could do.

"But forget all that. You can't uninvent the wheel, any more than you can unkill the mammoth or spit out the bug and hope it will live. And we've come so far with it now, I'd hate to see us have to reinvent the wheel. The wheel has so much to offer us, so much to give us. I know many of you said to me you loved the wheel. And when you said that, I showed you a little something to do tonight, so I want you to join with me and show me how much you love the wheel. Let's hear it for the wheel!"

Bug Lover started clapping. He clapped his hands together, palm to palm. Flat fingers against his palm. It made a loud noise. His lonely clapping echoed off the hills behind him. For a terrible moment he thought he was going to be the only one, but then a few others picked it up with him and then a few more, and soon what seemed like at least half the hillside was clapping. It was a fantastic noise, and it made Bug Lover's heart race.

The clapping died away. Moon Smacked and Bug Lover stood side by side and looked out at the crowd.

Skinny Bones stepped forward.

"I've been appointed by the log rollers to supervise the vote. Mainly because I'm one of the few who can count. As we decided, could those who like the wheel move to this side and those who don't move over there?"

While Moon Smacked and Bug Lover watched nervously, people started to move from one side to the other. The first ever vote in history was working.

A disturbance at the back of the crowd made them look up. Everyone was turning around.

Five very strange-looking people were making their way through the crowd toward Bug Lover and Moon Smacked. Smiling broadly, they came up to the pair of them.

"Hi!" said Quincy.

"Hello," said the kids. Feynman stood still and surveyed the crowd.

Bug Lover looked startled but decided to be courteous. "I don't think I've seen you lot before, but anyway, welcome. You're here for the vote?"

"Yip," said Quincy. "We wanted to see your buggy." He pointed at the cart.

"Oh, this little thing?" said Bug Lover. "Buggie? After me? I don't mind that." And then to cover up his pleasure he coughed and went into some technical description.

"Ahem. Four wheels all round, solid timber construction, two independent axles, front and back. Be the first in your tribe to get one. Maybe the first person anywhere," Bug Lover joked nervously, walking around his cart, flicking glances into the crowd and back at his strange new companions, hoping they wouldn't upset anything.

Skinny Bones stepped forward behind them. "I'm ready to count," he said. "Are you ready?" he asked Bug Lover and Moon Smacked.

They both nodded.

Quincy held up a hand. "I'm sorry. Do you mind if we just do one more little test? I really want to make sure it's safe. That it can't hurt anyone."

Quincy walked around the buggy and kicked the wheels.

"It's solid enough."

He pressed down a little on the front.

"You need to invent suspension, and it's really quite heavy."

Bug Lover nodded, only half-understanding what was going on.

"Gen?" called Quincy. "Could you go and stand just down that hill a bit. That's it. A bit farther. Farther. That ought to do it."

Quincy beckoned to Jules.

"Jules? Give this thing a big push and then ride it straight at Gen, will you?"

Jules grinned and nodded.

"What are you doing?" asked Bug Lover, somewhat concerned now that the strangers seemed to be all over his invention. Feynman grabbed him by the elbow, and he was unable to move.

Jules pulled the cart back to the other side of the clearing. It sloped quite steeply down toward where Gen was standing. The gathered tribes were silent. All eyes were on Jules.

He started pushing. The buggy gathered speed. As he felt it slipping away from him, he leapt onto it. His weight caused it to move even faster.

Gen. It's Gen. You're plummeting toward Gen. You can't do it, you can't do it, you can't do it!

Jules pushed himself up a little. He could see Gen standing there, waving at him. She didn't seem to mind what was happening.

Jules tucked his feet underneath him and crouched on the buggy as it bounced closer and closer to Gen.

No, Jules. No, Jules. I can't let you. You can't let you. You can't do this. You can't do this!

Jules stood up. He shifted his weight onto his back foot.

"Jules!" Gen called out in a happy voice.

Jules pressed down on his back foot, lifting the front wheels slightly off the ground. He twisted his body and the buggy moved an inch or two to the left, enough to send it hurtling past Gen and straight into a tree.

The buggy smashed into pieces and Jules flew on, narrowly missed the tree, and thudded into the ground. He lay still.

"Cool," said Gen.

"Can I have a go?" yelled Theo.

Bug Lover, Two Brow, and Star Speck ran down the hill to where Jules was lying. Behind them the vote had ceased. The men milled around, confused about what to do. A few changed sides, but most just sat down and waited for something to happen.

Bug Lover reached Jules and turned him over. He wasn't bleeding anywhere, but he wasn't responding, either.

From behind him Bug Lover could hear someone speaking. He turned around. He could see two figures standing back where the cart had been, and the shorter, fatter one was addressing the crowd.

"Listen to me!" said Quincy, and his voice was huge and terrifying. "I am the god of—ah, the god of—well, I'm God, all right? I have appeared before you tonight to tell you that the wheel is evil. Look at what it can do."

The god pointed down the hill to where Jules was lying. Bug Lover ran and hid.

"Reject the wheel! You are wrong to even think about it. No one needs it, and it offends me, God. So don't do it. You hear me?"

Quincy leaned over to Feynman.

"Go and get Jules. Pick him up, and we'll get out of here."

Feynman turned and headed down the hill.

The crowd stood transfixed in front of Quincy. They were terrified. Quincy had translated his speech into their language, and they truly believed that this was God, or at least *a* god.

But then to make them truly worried and very frightened, alongside Quincy appeared a skinny, tall, angry old man.

"You're not a god. You're a totally out of control megalomaniac," yelled Franklin.

Quincy sniggered.

"Look, Feynman. It's Franklin. Run and hide."

Feynman turned around. He had Jules in his arms. Gen and Theo came and stood by him.

"Quincy," said Franklin. "Enough! Time to stop. This isn't achieving anything!"

"You think?" said Quincy. "See, I disagree. I think this is much better than what I'd originally planned. And you know, I have you to thank for it. You kept pushing me. Really, I didn't know we had this kind of capability. By the time I'm finished, the past will be a blank program and I can Jump in and stimulate some evolution here, drop in an invention there. I'm going to reboot history with a whole new progam, and you're going to love it! Oh, except you're not in it. Too bad."

"That's what you think!" yelled Franklin. "You haven't done a thing. It's all on hold at MeanTime—"

"MeanTime! Duncan?" snorted Quincy. "I built that. Designed that system with him, you forget, you skinny old nuisance. It can't contain the ripples from everything we've done. We've dropped enough stones in this pond to empty it. Nothing is going to be the same ever again! Oh, hang on."

Quincy held up his hand. He was listening to his coat. He smiled at Franklin.

"Like I said, it's happening. Or it's unhappening. The wheel finished him off. Duncan's letting it all go.

245

Time is collapsing. Off we'll go, and start again. But better. You should have given me the kids."

"Time to go?" asked Feynman.

Quincy nodded. "Bye-bye." He waved.

And then they Jumped.

Jules fell to the ground and groaned. Gen looked like someone had just slapped her.

"Where are we?" asked Theo.

Franklin shook his head and stared at them. Gen ran over and grabbed him by the arm.

"What's happened, Franklin? Last I remember we'd caught up to Jules with those disgusting monkeys. Now we're here, where- and whenever this is."

Jules moaned some more and sat up.

"What is this site, Franklin? There's nothing here except those last few primitives running over the hill. We'd better go, hadn't we?"

Franklin slumped down to the ground. Theo came up close to him and gave him a shake.

"Franklin, come on! What's going on here? Let's go!"

"Forget it," said Franklin in a quiet flat voice. "There's nowhere to go to. Welcome to your new home. It's quite nice. You'll enjoy the taste of a juicy bug soon enough."

"Franklin, don't talk like that! Let's Jump, let's go."

Franklin looked up at Theo.

"You want to Jump? Go right ahead. It won't be there."

Theo grabbed his JumpMan out of his coat. It was dull and it didn't hover. It just fell onto the ground. He picked his remote out of his pocket and the screen was blank.

"Coat?" he called. "Coat!"

But his coat was just a piece of cloth hanging from his shoulders.

Theo's eyes widened. Gen stood next to him. Jules brought his aching head up to look at Franklin. No one said anything.

Franklin looked back at them.

"Quincy did it."

The silence of the surrounding forest was deep. Even the insects seemed still. The moon went behind a cloud. It was dark and deathly quiet.

"Quincy has made everything unhappen. Soon we might unhappen. Or we might suddenly find ourselves on the moon. Or we might suddenly not be here at all. Who knows? The time ripples of the unhappening are totally unpredictable. Quincy thinks he can control them. But he can't."

Franklin looked up at them. "Sorry, kids. We've lost. We couldn't do it. Sorry."

Franklin hung his head. Without saying anything or even noticing they were doing it, the three of them moved in close to one another. Jules felt Gen take his hand.

"O Key. Three kids, one skinny old guy. Shouldn't there be two more of you?" inquired a voice from behind them.

They turned around. They were looking at a young woman, maybe a few years older than they. She was wearing a fabulous skintight black suit with lights running all over it. Images came and went on the suit, not on screens but in the fabric of the suit itself.

"Negato. Eyeball three ados, one crusty. Interro now for missing two. Checkback." The woman was talking to someone else, but then she addressed a question to them.

"Anyone here called Feynman?"

"Feynman?" said Gen, astonished. "Who are you? How do you know about Feynman?"

"Ignoro that. He's been here?"

"Just gone!" said Theo.

The woman looked horrified.

"Ear up!" she snapped, back on the communications link. "Recheck on the TimeCoords. Minus 120 seconds and counting."

She paused for a second.

"O Key," she said, and she gave them all a brief smile, and then was gone.

"What in the known galaxy was that all about?" was about all Theo had time to say before the entire known galaxy around them began to spin in reverse.

He felt like he was being sucked backward through a washing machine on full cycle and then spat back out the other end. The forest whirled, the stars above him shook, Franklin stood up, Theo himself moved down the hill, and then all of a sudden it was like someone jammed on a brake.

In front of them stood Quincy. Feynman was next to him, again carrying Jules.

Franklin was yelling at him: "That's what you think! You haven't done a thing. It's all on hold at MeanTime—"

The three kids looked at one another. Hadn't Franklin yelled all that about a minute ago?

"MeanTime! Duncan?" snorted Quincy. "I built that. Designed that system with him, you forget, you skinny old nuisance. It can't contain the ripples from everything we've done. We've dropped enough stones in this pond to empty it. Nothing is going to be the same ever again! Oh, hang on."

This was really strange. This had all just happened, and now it was happening again.

Quincy held up his hand. He was listening to his coat. He smiled at Franklin.

"Like I said, it's happening. Or it's unhappening. The wheel finished him off. Duncan's letting it all go. Time is collapsing. Off we'll go, and start again. But better. You should have given me the kids."

"Time to go?" asked Feynman.

Quincy nodded. "Bye-bye." He waved.

And right then the script changed. In front of Feynman appeared the woman in the black suit.

"Feynman?" she asked.

Feynman raised an eyebrow.

The woman drew out a small bottle with an air bag and blower attached and blew a small pink cloud in Feynman's face.

Feynman sniffed and sneezed and dropped Jules. He then raised his right hand and began to dismantle his own head. He sped up, and in less than a minute there was nothing there at all.

"Ear up," barked the woman again. "Feynman finito. Time coords check out. ID all players. You Genevieve?" she asked, leaning down to make sure.

"Yes," said Gen, a little shocked at Feynman's sudden disappearance, at the rapid rewind she'd just experienced from the future she'd just lived through, and generally just a little surprised to be back here again and looking at a woman with bright yellow skin.

"Jules?" she asked, pointing at Jules, who was just coming around.

"What? Where am I? Who's she?" asked Jules. "Hey, I can talk! Where's Feynman?" Jules felt a rush of incredible relief. "I'm back!" he shouted. "What's happened?"

"Theo, Franklin," the woman said. "So you must be Quincy Carter One."

Quincy backed away a little.

The woman was intimidating, and his image had just appeared on her suit scrolling along with data.

"Nice outfit," he said nervously.

"Quincy Carter One, I charge you under the Cause and Effect Act of Fourteen Billion Eight Hundred and Sixty-four with one hundred and twenty-three acts of time manipulation and chrono dislodgement. I order you to hand over your JumpMan and come with me."

Gen looked up, frowning. "You said Fourteen Billion Eight Hundred and Sixty-four?"

"Affirmo," said the woman.

"You're from the future?"

"Well, that's all relative, but affirmo."

Gen nodded quickly. "Eight hundred years ahead of Quincy and Theo?"

"Do you have to keep going on about this?"

The woman shuffled her feet and looked a little embarrassed.

"Look, my name's Ivana Qroca. Um, we would have got here sooner, but you know what time can be like. It takes its time. Nothing happens till the time is right—"

"Quincy!" yelled Franklin.

But Quincy wasn't there. He'd gone. Quincy had Jumped.

"Ear up," Ivana barked. "We've got an Alpha 478. TimeLock on JumpMan belonging to a Quincy Ethel Carter One. Last seen heading in a pre-fourteenth-billennium direction. All units, checkback with coords."

Ivana looked around at them. "It's O Key. We'll find him."

"Who are you?" asked Jules.

"Yeep, well, it's a long story. About eight hundred years long, really. You see, Quincy actually won. He made everything unhappen all right. There's been eight hundred years in which Quincy was master of the universe, created a whole race of Feynmans, took over Mars, sent probes out to all the nearest stars . . . Anyway, I won't bore you. He got everything he wanted. But there was a little pocket of resistance on Mars. Your parents," she said, pointing at Jules and Gen.

"Our parents?" they both said together. Ivana nodded.

"Your parents and Cynthia. They were trapped in a ChronoCage, and they escaped and formed the Resistance. They were the last living memory of what things had been like before Quincy went through the past like a maniac and destroyed everything."

This was starting to sound really weird.

"They formed a gang, and—don't be shocked—they had a few more kids, and their descendants carried on the secret work. We wanted to find out what had happened and when, and we did. About four hundred years ago."

She stopped, looking embarrassed.

"I'm sorry about this but over the last four hundred years we've been having a very long discussion about what we should do. Rule One. Can you go back and change history? Quincy had changed history but maybe that's what was meant to happen. But then another whole group argued that he wasn't meant to change history so it would be all right to go back and change the moment when he changed it. But then we'd argue that if it wasn't right to change history then it would be wrong to go back and change history even if you were changing it to make sure it didn't change."

"But you're here." Franklin spoke up for the first time in a long while.

"I'm part of a secret radical group. It's called Cut the Talking. We decided to see what would happen if we did something for once."

"What did you do to Feynman?" asked Jules.

"Blew a virus in his face. He was a computer. The virus reprogrammed each of his nanos to turn off the nano next to it. Worked pretty well, I thought."

"And Quincy?" asked Gen.

"Coords coming through right now. Here you go. Go get him!"

Ivana pulled a tiny thin sliver of metal from a pocket on her suit.

"That a JumpMan?" asked Theo.

"JumpMan Pro X. Nice model. Wouldn't mind the mini version though."

She hit the GoButton and then disapppeared.

"Wait!" yelled Theo, and Ivana reappeared.

"Yeep?" she asked.

"What's going to happen? Is everything going to be back in place? Can we still TimeJump?"

"Can't tell you. Rule One, you know. This was bad enough. Gotta go. Got to find out if I still exist. Bye!"

Ivana disappeared.

Franklin leapt to his feet, reenergized and ready to go.

"Shall we?" he shouted happily. "Got those coords,

Gen? I bet I know where he's gone, anyway. Let's go."

They all closed their eyes and Jumped.

Bug Lover poked his head back over the top of the hill. One by one the intruders had all vanished in front of him. He stared at the spot where they'd been. Then he flipped over onto his back and stared up at the sky. He counted the stars, he studied the moon, he smelled the rich smell of the night all around him. Then he put his hands under his head and smiled a deep satisfied smile, as though everything had just become clear to him. He was right about the wheel.

His friend Ochre Boy, who'd made the wonderful paintings of Two Brow's family on horseback, made a series of very popular paintings about the night. Thousands of years later they were still being studied, and many people had all sorts of theories about the modern-looking figures standing around and the small hovering spheres near their heads.

THE PAST
DAYTIME, PRECAMBRIAN ERA, 380 MILLION YEARS AGO

They opened their eyes. Small pools of water steamed in shallow rock hollows. A brown sea the color of

French onion soup lapped at the edge of smooth orange rocks. The air smelled strange, and bits of yellow smoke curled up from cracks around them.

Quincy was standing in the shallows just in front of them.

"Come to watch the end of everything, have you?" he bellowed at them.

"Why don't you just leave me alone? One little thing is all I ask, and you keep chasing me and chasing me and forcing me to do things like this. It's you, Franklin! You and those brats tagging along with you. You that's doing this, not me!"

"Yes, Quincy," said Franklin, looking a little bored with it all.

"Where are we?" asked Jules.

"Good question," said Franklin. "Where are we, Quincy?"

"The start of it all! This is it! It all starts here and now! Or rather, it did all start here and now, and soon it's about to end here and now. There'll be no here and now. Just then. Just what used to be. Your fault! You can stop it, if you like, Franklin. Up to you!"

Quincy was really screaming. Not that there was anyone or anything to hear him apart from Theo, Jules, Gen, and Franklin.

"We are a very long way back, aren't we?" said Gen.

"No birds, no beach, brand-new rocks. I'd say, thirteenth billennium?" suggested Theo.

"Not bad," said Franklin. "Have you found what I think you've found, old Quince?"

"Wip, of course! I find whatever I want to find. I'm not some clumsy TimeFumbler like yourself, sending kids off to fall out of the sky and maybe they'll see a prehistoric giraffe! Phiff!" Quincy snorted. "You always thought so small, Franklin! Even just a few changes to history and I could have got us all to an incredible level. I could have been the beginning of it all. The beginning of a revolution. A civilization that could improve its chances by correcting its mistakes. What's wrong with that?"

Quincy stomped around in the shallows. "I mean, that's where I started. But then the last few months—ever since Theo disappeared, what an education. I could have plotted a whole new course for humanity. Started everything earlier. Lent a hand when it was needed. Think what kind of life we might have been leading by Fourteen Billion and Seventy-three. But no, you think we've just got to plod through our past like we always have, the past is gone—well it isn't, you know. We're standing in it. And we can change it."

Quincy kicked at the water, and some of it splashed

on Jules. He got a taste of something very strange. Not salty, not fresh, more like he imagined acid might taste. He hoped it wasn't poisonous.

"So, I'm sick of trying. I'm sick of it all. I'm sick of trying to help you all. To lead you into the promised land. If you don't want it, I don't want it. I don't want any of it."

Quincy held up his hand, and they could see he was holding a small piece of glass like a microscope slide.

"You found it then?" called out Franklin. "You got the very first piece of DNA there?"

"This is it, you sad old reboot," Quincy yelled back. "The very first piece of DNA. All the little molecules swimming about here have just made themselves into a little piece of DNA, and it is so eager to replicate itself. It can't wait. It's like a kid with a JuniorJumper. But you know what? I'm going to pull it apart. I'm not going to let it. And when I do, phip, good night!"

Quincy waved the slide about as though he were drunk, spun around, and fell over in the water.

"What's he going to do?" asked Gen.

"He's got the first DNA—always been a bit of a prize site, if you could find it. Proves the whole thing, and you see, all life is descended from the one bit of DNA that was so keen to keep going that it started to create structures to keep itself alive. We're just complex life-support systems to keep the DNA going."

"We are?" said Jules.

"If you want a particularly bleak view of the world, yes," said Franklin.

"Shouldn't we stop him?" suggested Gen. "I mean, if he's going to rip it apart, and we're all going to disappear, wouldn't it be a good idea to stop him?"

"Oh, I don't know," said Franklin. "Aren't you interested to see what might happen? If he's right, then it will be as if we never existed. That's fascinating, isn't it? The ultimate outcome of evolution is that it creates something that goes back and destroys itself before it can begin? I'm quite interested to see if that's the case."

"I'm not," yelled Jules. "What's got into you? We come all this way and, at the very end, we let him win because it might be interesting?" Jules yelled this as he ran forward over the rocks and into the sea.

"Too late!" screamed Quincy. "I'm doing it now!"

He whipped the top off the glass slide, pulled a silver rod from his pocket, activated it, and a green laser beam shot out at the slide.

"Ha!" he cried. "It's done. Say good-bye, forever!" And he threw his arms up into the air, a triumphant look on his face.

Quincy held that pose for quite a while. Jules

splashed through the shallows and grabbed him and knocked the slide out of his hand. Quincy jumped up and down a few more times, but his victory shouts became a little quieter.

Some blue gray clouds rolled overhead. Some particularly spectacular lightning split the sky. The brown sea lapped the shore. Jules became aware of the deep silence. When you go back to before life was created, there are none of the sounds of life. No city noise, no rustle of wind in the trees, no waving of the grass, no squawk of birds.

That's a plus, said his brain.

What is?

No birds. No seagulls. Hate seagulls. At least you could eat chips here and there'd be no flying rats to annoy you. But then there'd be no chips, either. Which came first, do you think? The chip or the seagull?

Jules forgot to tell his brain to go away.

Quincy's arms had come down by his sides. "Any minute now," he said with not much conviction. "The undoing of Life, the unhappening of it all, probably takes a few minutes. There's a lot to undo."

"Oh, I don't think so," said Franklin. "It would be instantaneous. Are you sure you got the first piece of DNA? Not the second? Or maybe the twenty-seventh?"

Quincy's shoulders slumped. "It's coming," he said. "You wait."

But his voice was very quiet, and after another minute or two he was still just standing there, looking wet and sad.

"Come on, Quincy," said Franklin. "You should have figured that out. Doesn't matter if you get the first piece. The second piece of DNA will do the same thing. You've got an ocean of molecules. They're all heading in the same direction. And then whichever bit of DNA does it first, it's swimming around in exactly the same conditions. Doesn't matter if it happens today or next Tuesday. You're still going to end up two billion years later with creatures like us that know it's Tuesday."

Franklin smiled at Quincy. "And if you'd destroyed the very basis of life," said Franklin, "how would you have evolved to be you and come and destroy the very basis of life?"

Quincy sighed, "There're more of them, aren't there?"

Franklin nodded.

"Whole sea full of molecules, desperate to get together and become DNA. They can't wait. These guys are keen!"

Franklin waved his arms about at the ocean and the rocks and the steaming pools around them. "Look at where we are, Quincy. We are two billion years ago. There is no today or tomorrow. The calendar hasn't even started yet. DNA starts today and it's still going to take four hundred million years to become slime. Plenty of time, Quincy."

Quincy slumped down onto his knees in the shallow water.

"You knew you couldn't change the future because it hasn't happened yet," continued Franklin. "You knew you couldn't change the present because it never happens. But you can't change the past, either. The past is always someone else's future. All you can do, Quincy, is live. Live in your own TimeFlow. Be. Exist. Choose. Nothing else going on, here or in Fourteen Billion and Seventy-three or in fourteen billion years after that."

A deep silence settled over everything. Jules thought Franklin looked very old but very wise.

"Quincy, you and I go back a long way. But you've been wrong. You've been wrong for a hundred years. And now it's over. Come on back and help us fix everything up. Lot of work to do. Wanna help?"

Franklin held out his hand to Quincy, but Quincy backed away, a wild look in his eye.

"Huh, zif!" he snorted. "I'm staying here. I'm going anywhere I want to go. I'm still the only one who gets the full potential of TimeJumping, and it's not Jumping in to watch people flap about and make the same mistakes over and over again. It's to make the human race the most powerful force in the universe. It's to reach our potential. If we can do it, then we are meant to do it! Don't you see that? Applestickers! Moon drones! Beltheads!"

Quincy stomped off, splashing water around, yelling and waving his arms about wildly.

"Oak-I," called out Franklin. "See you later, then. Good luck. You sure? We'll be off, then."

Quincy ignored them.

Franklin shrugged. "Come on. Let's go," he said.

"You're just going to leave him here?" asked Theo. "We finally track him down, and we're going to leave him again?"

"Nip, nip, nip, nothing to worry about," said Franklin. "Duncan's put a TimeTag on his JumpMan. He can't go anywhen without setting off alarms. Anyway, he'll be hungry in about an hour. What's he going to eat a billion years before there's even some decent algae?"

They came in close, checked the settings on their JumpMans, closed their eyes, and Jumped.

chapter eight
TIME HONORED

THE FUTURE

FRIDAY AFTERNOON FOURTEEN BILLION AND

SEVENTY-THREE

They were all back in the United Planets grow tower.

A tall woman, in a shimmering grape-colored dress that moved around her like small clouds, walked toward them. She was talking into a light shawl draped perfectly over her shoulders.

"Why would I want to do that? I was going to get new elbow skin at about four this afternoon, and then I thought we might all go ski the Mons. Can you hold on one moment? Hello, Gen."

The tall woman bent down and kissed Gen on the cheek.

"Mom?" said Gen.

"Darling. Don't you just adore Mars?"

"But, Mom, you were trapped."

"We were? Is this some game you're playing? Look, got to go, they're trying to make us go back to Earth and, even worse, back to Mil 3. Personally I'm all for staying here, and your father is meeting with President Mavis about it right now. Better go—see you for some prots and carbs a bit later . . ."

Katherine shimmered off.

"She looks fantastic," said Jules.

"Franklin, what happened to her?"

"Well, your parents were in a ChronoCage, and then in one version of events they escaped and led the revolution. But after Ivana Jumped in and put time back in place, it's like you've all been having a fabulous holiday on Mars. Your parents have adapted to it remarkably quickly."

"Jules!"

Tony Santorini zipped in and hovered next to Jules in a BodyCar.

"Can you believe this thing? I am not going back to Mil 3 and my rusty 1989 Camry. I'm staying here with this thing. Do you know, all you have to do is help out every day to maintain the whole place and everything is available for free? Gotta love Mars, Jules. You want to stay? Is that the time? Gotta go—I'm playing Octo-Tennis. See you for bits and vits later. Bye."

Gen, Jules, and Theo all looked at one another.

"What's happened to our parents?"

"They've never been like this before."

"Are we going to have to stay? Here on Mars?" asked Gen. "I wouldn't mind going home."

"You can't stay," replied Franklin. "You have to go back and live your lives. Otherwise, Mars doesn't happen. That reminds me. There is something here I'd like you two to see before you go."

And he whistled up a couple of BodyCars. Franklin, Jules, and Gen got in and zapped off, with Franklin leading. They skimmed rapidly through the grow towers and out onto the plains of carb grass, punctuated by lakes of aquatofu and forests of protbush. The sun was setting quickly, and the greenish sky was streaked with dark blue. Mars's moons were not yet up, and the stars came out quite quickly, but Jules and Gen still had plenty of time to admire the view: the rolling blues of the carbgrass, the deep purples and white of the aquatofu lakes, the meat-red colors of the protbush forests.

BodyCars filled the skies, and grow tower cities were everywhere, with everything tidy and just so. The group banked to the right, screeched in behind a hill, and came to a stop. Jules unzipped himself from his BodyCar. Franklin was already out and stomping up a small rise in front of them. And oddly enough, in this valley it did seem as though things had been allowed to run a little wild. Blue carb grass grew in thick tussocks and hummus weed was spreading out and decomposing at an incredibly fast rate. Gen had to leap out of its way. Prot bushes were dropping what looked like lumps of mince, and some of them were starting to rot. The place stank.

There was no path to the top. Franklin was leaping from tussock to tussock of carb grass, and Jules and Gen came up behind him, trying to avoid the hummus weed whacking them on the ankles.

They reached the top and gazed up at the stars, out now and shining their distant light down on them. Franklin was rushing about, poking under prot bushes, kicking away leaves and twigs, and tearing back at the hummus weed. As usual, he was muttering to himself.

"I'm sure this is it. I'm sure this is the hill. Can't be anywhere else."

"What can't be anywhere else?" asked Gen.

Franklin straightened up, and something like a smile crossed his face. He reached out to stroke Gen's hair, became flustered, and ended up giving her a slap on the ear.

He turned away and continued searching and muttering. He strode about kicking up more twigs, branches, leaves, and hummus in various stages of decay. Then he tripped over something and fell flat on his face.

"Found it!" he yelled, his voice a little muffled because his mouth was down in the dirt. Jules and Gen ran over to him. Franklin was sitting up and pointing to something at his feet.

Jules could see what looked like part of a wall. A few feet of it were still visible; the rest he assumed disappeared under the ground. There was a flat piece of metal attached to the wall like a plaque.

"Read it!" he ordered. "Jules, get in there and get the dirt off it."

The metal had rusted and there were plants growing all over it. Jules pulled them back and then rubbed at the dirt with his hand.

"We've got to see this?" he asked.

Franklin nodded.

The dirt came away, and Jules could see some letters. He pulled his sleeve over his fist and gave the plaque a harder scrub. Gen came over and knelt beside him. They leaned over to make out the writing on the plaque and then both snapped back up.

"Where did it come from?"

"How long's it been here?"

They fired off questions rapidly, eyes staring wide at Franklin.

"How did you find out about this?"

He laughed and held up his hands. "Only just done it. I could not figure out why Quincy was so interested in you. So I fed everything about you into the info-mine. Came up with this. In the first years of Mars occupation there was a school built here. And they called it Rosemount High. I knew that rang a data chip somewhere, so I tracked it down."

"There were schools on Mars?"

"Everyone on Mars came from Earth. They brought Earthlife with them. They terraformed as they went and built little remakes of Earth everywhere. The early maps of Mars are the best guide to what Earth used to be like. So, yip, there were schools."

Jules and Gen bent down again to read the plaque and take it in:

ROSEMOUNT HIGH
THIS SCHOOL IS DEDICATED TO THE
MEMORY OF JULES ENRICO SANTORINI
AND GENEVIEVE JOANNE CORRIGAN.
WITHOUT THEM, NOTHING.

Jules wished they hadn't put his full name on there. "Enrico" came from a grandfather he never knew, and he tried to keep it quiet. Now he felt like all of Mars must have been laughing at him.

"Without Them, Nothing," Gen repeated a few times. It was hard to believe.

Jules dug down a little farther.

"Oh my God," he said. "Read this."

OPENED ON THIS DAY
BY JULES SANTORINI,
2 JULY 2098

Jules stared at it for a while. He was remembering an old man on a spacecraft. An old man with his name sitting next to an old woman called Gen.

"We come here," he said to Franklin. "We grow up and when we are very old we come to Mars. With everyone else."

"Yes, you do. It's taken me a long time to find you. To find out anything about you. Because it could never have been an accident that Theo jumped into your room, Gen. He picked up the wrong JumpMan and that was its pre-set. Quincy was getting ready to come and see you. He may have already been there."

"But why?" said Gen. "Why would come and see us?"

Franklin nodded and smiled. "Time's a funny thing,"

he said, echoing something Jules had been thinking for some months now. "We are living a version of events that results from Theo picking up the wrong JumpMan and coming to your place. He picks up the wrong JumpMan because Quincy has programmed it in order to try and stop him from Jumping to your place. But he only Jumps to your place because Quincy tries to stop him Jumping there."

It was falling into place in Jules's head. He'd become so used to these circular and twisted time arguments that he could see where this one was going. He picked up the argument.

"Because Theo jumps into our time and meets us, I end up going off into the Future and meeting myself as an old man."

"What?" said Gen. "When did that happen? Why haven't you told me that?"

"I . . . it was too much. I could hardly make sense of it myself."

Franklin continued. "You see yourself, you live all this, you come to the future. You go back to your present and you begin to work to make this future happen. You're not the leaders of the movement to evacuate Earth. But both of you work in a way that makes it happen. Quincy went about undoing history by attacking

Edison and Newton and some of the big hitters. But sometimes it's not them that really matter. Could you stop Columbus from sailing by jamming him in jail? Or by stopping boats from being designed? Sails from being invented? By getting rid of whoever in the court of Spain thought it would be fun to send him off?"

Franklin smiled at them both.

"You two aren't Columbus. In fact, Gen, what you do—"

"No!" shouted Gen, leaping at Franklin and shoving him in the chest before he had a chance to speak. "Don't tell us."

She stood over Franklin. "I don't want to know. I don't want to know any more. That's enough. It's too much. Whatever happens after this, I just want it to happen. I don't want to wake up every day knowing what it is I'm going to do. It's too much."

Gen sat down and hung her head in her hands. She could feel that she wanted to cry, but she also felt too angry and frustrated to do it properly. Maybe later, back in her room. For now, she'd had enough. She wanted to go.

"What about you, Jules?" asked Franklin. "Enough?"

Oh, please, get him to tell us.

No!

Don't be crazy! Aren't you just dying to know?

Yes. No . . . Oh, I don't know.

I do. Ask him! Ask him!

Jules stood up from scraping away at the plaque. After a moment he nodded.

"Enough. Gen's right. Whatever we end up doing, we have to go back and just live it out. We can't know. It's Rule One, isn't it?"

Franklin smiled. This time it was warm and genuine.

"Well done, TimeJumper. You don't really understand something just by doing what you're told. You understand it when you have to make a choice. There are no JumpSites in the future, because life can't be lived like that. The past is gone, the present never happens, the future is unknown. That's just it, and that's the way it must always be. There may be places and times out there that are different, but not here, not now. Here, it's Rule One all the way down and back again."

Franklin smiled and this time managed to give them both a hug that was almost affectionate.

"Franklin, what is Rule One?" asked Gen. "It's not just 'Don't Touch Anything,' is it?"

Franklin nodded at Gen. "Well done, you," he replied. Franklin looked out from the hill and up at the stars.

"Rule One is about everything. Everything is in the universe, the universe is in everything. Don't Touch

Anything? That was just the simplest way of putting it so everyone could understand. Don't touch, don't tell, don't interfere. Don't change anything. You can't, anyway. We're talking about space and time, and that's the universe. It starts as a single tiny point, it unfolds, it finishes, and you know what?"

Gen and Jules didn't say anything. Franklin was kind of glowing in the night light and needed no encouragement. All of his cranky ways were gone and he was speaking easily, his voice full of joy.

"Nothing you can do about it. It is, it shall be, it will be again. All you can do is wonder. Wonder at the beauty of it all. Wonder at yourself and your place in it. You can spend your whole life wondering and asking and seeking the answers to it all, and you know what? At the end you'll know as much as you did when you were burbling in your bassinet. All you can do is wonder. Wonder at your understanding, wonder at your own wondering. We are a wonder as is all life, both here and beyond. That's Rule One."

Jules felt like he'd been listening to incredible music, or as though he'd drunk some tonic. He felt lighter and refreshed. He looked at Gen, and she took his hand and smiled.

"So what do we do now?" he asked.

"Do?"

"Do. We go back home and then what do we do?"

Franklin put a hand on Jules's shoulder. "You do the only thing anyone can do. You live your life. Do whatever you want to do. Whatever it is you are meant to do, you'll do it. People worry too much. You are a part of life, Jules, and you, Gen. Rule One. You can't change life, because life is as life is. We've run like rabid goats from one end of time to the other, and everything has turned out as it turned out. Quincy nearly succeeded but eventually—it took a while, I'll grant you—eventually everything turned out, and soon we will all be where we were before anything happened.

"The universe rights itself. The past is gone, the present never happens, and the future is unknown. You'll go home, resume life in your own TimeFlow, and you'll be fine. Whatever you do, it will be important. It will also not matter very much at all."

Jules and Gen digested that information. Franklin had managed to make them feel connected to the entire sweep of the universe and very insignificant at the same time.

"You're connected to the beginning of time and the end of time," said Franklin, as if he'd been reading their thoughts. "We all are. You know how the nanobots take matter and make things? They're just doing what the universe has been doing since time began and will do until time ends. Everything you're made of was there at the beginning and everything that will be made is in you right now. It goes on until it ends."

"And then it starts again?" said Gen.

"Then it starts again," said Franklin.

They all stood for a moment, looking at the plaque, looking out at the view, and feeling their own bodies and minds reaching upward into the endless black of space.

"Better go," said Franklin, and they turned and walked back down to the BodyCars.

"So you're both agreed?" he asked as they zipped themselves in.

"Can't be one without the other. You have to both want to do this."

Jules and Gen nodded without looking at each other.

Franklin switched on the BodyCars, and the little convoy rose and shot back toward the United Planets grow tower.

A few days later Jules, Gen, and Theo stood quietly in a reception hall with nothing much to say to one another. There was nothing to fight about, nothing to rescue, nothing to plan. They were with Mavis the Prez in the

United Planets grow tower. Jules watched the rich colors glowing and pulsating off other grow towers across the plain, and the steady lines of BodyCars winding among them. Gen wandered slowly from wallslide to wallslide, reading the captions and occasionally, without much caring either way, blinking up more. Theo tried to start up a conversation with both of them, but it was soon obvious they weren't in a chatty mood. He sat down and began playing Asteroid Belt on his coat.

Cynthia ran in ahead of Steven and Katherine.

"I Jumped! I Jumped! I went to JuniorJumpers, and we've been to the gold rush!"

Steven and Katherine came in, both looking vibrant and freshly scrubbed.

"Great workout," declared Steven, stretching. He'd really taken to the AirPool and was now doing fifty laps every afternoon at quite intense pressures.

Katherine had been having a Martian dust bath. Early Mars dwellers found that Mars had places with thermal dust—hot dust heated by escaping underground heat. The Martians kept a few when they terraformed, and these spots were now the place to go for relaxation and some bodywork. The client is rotated in hot dust, which cleanses the epidermis, unclogs the pores, rejuvenates the—well, that's what it says on the coat ads. It really just meant you felt great when you were lying in it, and it was a terrific excuse to do nothing for a few hours.

As well as falling in love with BodyCars, Tony had been spending time in the water mines. He'd never seen anything like the scale of the work.

"They can extract water from ice particles trapped between specks of dust. It's incredible!"

Angela was the last to arrive. She hadn't really enjoyed Mars. It was a very practical planet. People who were totally focused on survival and maintaining an artificial biosphere and atmosphere didn't have a lot of time left over for the spiritual world. And with most diseases and illnesses treated with transplants and spare parts, there was no alternative healing, as everybody was healed.

"I expected deeper resonance," said Angela. "I thought we might find a connection to the cosmos. But you can't hear the music of the universe over the sound of Martians bragging about themselves."

The grown-ups gathered around their children. Tony was the first to notice the mood.

"You lot all right? Jules?" he asked.

Jules gave his father a small tight smile and then turned away. Katherine looked inquiringly at Gen, who wouldn't meet her eye.

A wall slid back, and President Mavis and Franklin

came in. Jules, Gen, and Theo almost didn't recognize him. He was relaxed, had on a clean coat, and appeared to have had a shower in recent days.

"Gen, Jules, everyone, I'm glad to see you all back." Mavis's smile warmed the room. "When you came here, we treated you as aliens and enemies. I'm sorry, but I hope you can comprehend now how threatened we were. If I understand Franklin correctly, there has been a future where none of us existed anymore at all, and Quincy remade the worlds to his own design. That future is now behind us, thanks to you."

Jules looked down at his feet, and both Theo and Gen went red with embarrassment. The parents looked a little shocked.

"We owe you an incredible debt," President Mavis continued. "Without you, Quincy would have continued to slash his way through history, and crucial events would have continued to unhappen. Whatever the danger, you three just Jumped and Jumped and kept on confronting every single situation that was thrown at you. Well done!"

Gen and Jules smiled awkward little smiles. Really, they thought, we just tagged along. In fact, we made things worse.

"I know what you're thinking. You helped Quincy.

But actually you didn't. Your involvement brought your parents here, brought Franklin back, brought—well, it brought a whole lot of forces into play that made possible the eventual defeat of Quincy, and it enabled time to be put back."

"Where is he now?"

"Here. Our best chronopsychs are working on him, and we may have a reasonable human being one day soon."

Tony spoke up. "This is all very interesting, but what are you talking about?"

"Yes, well, Tony, I could explain, but if I told you that in a previous future you never left Mars, you stayed here, joined the rebels, and a descendant of yours eventually decided to go back and help Jules and Gen, would that help you at all? I doubt it, because right now you only remember what has happened since time was put back. Thanks in no small way to the efforts of your children—"

"Excuse me," interrupted Katherine, "but I can't even get Gen to put her clothes back where they belong. Are you sure it was her?"

"Yes, I am positive it was her. We are in the process of heading back to what should have happened before Quincy started to fool around with everything. There's a whole other future that you should be very glad is now not the future at all, but was the future when Quincy started making everything unhappen. Now it's all happening when it should, and everything's happening before everything else, just as it did before, and it's even better this time around!"

Katherine considered Mavis for a moment or two, thought about asking a question, and then decided she didn't want to show she had no idea what Mavis was talking about.

"There's nothing we can give you," said President Mavis, "to say thank you. Nothing we can really do that will have any meaning, but for this moment now, I want you to know that here in Fourteen Billion and Seventy-three, we'll never forget you."

Jules and Gen looked down at the floor. Jules felt his face go hot and his eyes start pricking.

Please stop me crying, he begged his brain.

You're not crying. You're allergic to praise.

Jules laughed at that, sniffed, and felt as though he could raise his head up.

Franklin stepped forward and put a hand on Jules's shoulder.

"It's time," he said quietly.

"Jules?" whispered Tony. "What's going on?"

"Shh, Dad, it doesn't matter." And he turned to

Theo. With all their self-consciousness gone, they hugged each other tightly. Theo and Jules broke apart and looked at each other, smiling deeply.

"Hey, Applesticker," said Jules. "Been nice knowing you."

Suddenly Theo had to brush something out of his eye.

"You too, Dodoboy."

Gen kissed Theo.

Uh-oh.

Oh, come on, brain, as if it matters now.

Jules realized he didn't feel jealous at all.

Theo blushed and smiled at Gen. "I can't come and see you again."

"I don't want you to. Even though I want you to," said Gen.

Jules cleared his throat. He felt someone should make a little speech.

"Mavis? Franklin, Theo. Mom and Dad and everyone. Um, for us it's been incredible to see everything we've seen, to be part of all of this, and even though I know we've got to do this, I think there'll still be something in all of us that will remember and be different just because we've known you all and been part of all of this."

Tony spoke up. "Jules, what are you talking about? What do they have to do?"

"It's Rule One, Dad. We have to forget."

"Forget?"

"They're going to make us forget. In a moment they'll do a TimeSweep, then Jump us, and we won't remember any of this."

"Won't remember?" said Tony. "How could we possibly forget coming to the future and going to Mars?"

"You're being ridiculous," said Katherine. "As if I won't remember getting new skin."

"You're going to forget it," said Gen. "It's happened to you before. And this time it's going to happen to us, too. It has to. Quincy wanted us because of something we do when we grow up. We don't know what it is, but we have to do it. If we remember all this, we're not going to grow up as we should, we'll be completely different, and it might mean we don't do what we were meant to do if none of this had ever happened. Can't take the risk."

Franklin and President Mavis went around and shook everyone by the hand.

The parents started to argue and protest. The children just hugged each other one last time and then stood patiently.

Franklin held up a TimeSweeper, there was a flash, and in the same moment everyone Jumped back to where it had all begun.

chapter nine
TIME PLEASE

THE PRESENT

FRIDAY NIGHT EARLY MIL 3

Time. *Time's a funny thing,* thought Jules. Is there ever really any break with the past? Or is the past always with us? Should you put your past behind you? Or keep it in front where you can see it?

Aren't we thoughtful? said his brain. *You know you should stop thinking about all this stuff and just focus on what you came here to do.*

I don't want to.

I know you don't want to. And that's why all the thinking about Time.

Since when did you care about time?

Jules slowly climbed the stairs, dragging one foot up after the other. His brain was right. He didn't want to think about what he was about to do.

From downstairs he could hear the sound of his father cracking jokes with Steven. They'd only just moved back and this was the first time they'd been over to see the Corrigans.

He knocked on Gen's door.

"Come in!" she yelled.

"Hey, Julie, Julie," she shrieked, leaping up from her bed, running across the room, and hugging him tightly. She kissed him and then moved back.

"Look at you," she said. "Long time."

"Been a while," said Jules. "You're old."

"You're fat!" she replied, pushing him over.

They both laughed.

Laughing. Laughing is good. I think this is going well.

Not now, brain. Go away.

His brain went away.

"So, have you climbed up to my castle to ask me out?" teased Gen.

"Nah," replied Jules. "I thought we might just stay right here. You never know what might turn up."

"Or who," Gen said, and smiled.

Jules smiled too.

"Or who," he agreed.